Cora vs. the Forces of Evil

Joshua Morgan

Contents

Chapter 1

It was supposed to be a normal day.Let me backtrack a little: My name is Cora and it had started out as a normal day. The sun rose, my cat, Church, woke me up for attention when my alarm rang, I got ready for school and was out the door twenty minutes later. I managed to stay awake and coherent in my classes and just prayed for the monotony to be over soon so I could go home. After my mom picked me up from school in her old Ford Taurus, we drove to the bank."I have to talk to someone about opening a new account. Can you go to the store over there and grab some stuff for dinner?" She asked. The bank in question was inside the Walmart, settled in between a nail salon and a bagged ice freezer. I nodded and set off on my journey to locate an acceptable frozen pizza. Since my parents had divorced about two months ago, my mom got custody of me and my dad got custody of my beautiful german shepherd, Mouse. Adopting Church was my mom's way of trying to help me accept the change of being separated from them both. But, I'm getting off-task. I walked over to the store, wrapping my black jacket tighter around myself against the chill of the air conditioner that was permanently set to meat locker temperature. It was the usual kind of Tuesday crowd hiding from the humid world outside. I didn't make eye contact with anybody while I looked around for the food when I was jostled by somebody running into my arm. "Oh, excuse me, sorry-" I was cut off by the tall, thin lady pressing something circular to my back. I froze, knowing instantly it was a gun. She leaned down to my ear and whispered. "You're going to drop what you're doing and walk normally. I will shoot if you cause any trouble." My thoughts picked up speed as I tried to keep control. Everything slowed down around me like someone had hit the .50x speed on a YouTube video and my brain kicked into hyperdrive.

SING. Use SING. Scream. Run. Don't let her take you to a second location.

I turned abruptly, knocked the barrel of the gun away and screamed "I don't know you!" while stomping as hard as I could onto her foot with the heel of my boot. The pistol skittered away on the ground as she registered what was happening. When she doubled over in pain, I went for the stomach and nose to put her on the ground while I straightened up, panting. Other shoppers started yelling and I thought they were going to come help when I heard a loud sound like a tire had been popped. A solid thud hit a wall and the screaming got louder.Being from Texas, I knew a gunshot when I heard it. People were running around and ducking under things in a general state of panic when my gaze settled on the woman who had tried to threaten me. She was tall and looked like she had peaked in the high school cheer team. She looked to weigh about 160 pounds of pure Texas beef, which was ironic because she was currently nursing a bleeding nose while ignoring the pistol on the ground. I dove for it and ran to the fitting rooms, the closest shelter. As I shut the door, I heard a voice on the intercom system break through the trashy pop music they were playing."Would the resident police officer please come to the front desk immediately?"Uh oh.

I peeked over the wall of the dressing rooms and got an eyeful of the drama. In my sight alone, there were three men armed to the teeth who were fighting the cashiers into the hair salon off to the side. I gulped and pulled out my phone to call 9-1-1.

"9-1-1, what's your emergency?" A man's voice answered calmly.

"Walmart on State Street. My name is Cora Locke and there is a hostage situation with at least three men. They have guns and they're shooting." Address first, as mom had always said."Where are you, Cora?" He asked, the sounds of his quick typing sounding through the line.

"In the dressing rooms. Please send help fast." I looked up at the sound of another shot. "Oh my god, they've shot the resident officer."

"Help is on the way. Ma'am, can you see if anyone else is injured?" The man responded, concern rising in his voice. I craned my neck to look before ducking back down. "I can't see anyone else. How long until help gets here?" I whispered, terrified that they would hear me. "ETA is five minutes. Can you give a description?" Calming enough to keep my voice from shaking, I answered him. "Three at least. They're all wearing ski masks and gloves. They moving into the bank, now." I quietly tiptoed over and shut the light switch off to put me in the dark. "My mom is in there." My hands were trembling.

"We're on our way. Stay on the line as long as you can." "Yes, sir." I tucked my phone under the little table in the wall that rested under the mirror and went absolutely still as I heard footsteps. There was a knock on my door and my heart threatened to beat out of my chest with fear. "Daddy? Where are you?" A little voice whispered. I opened the door and saw a small boy wearing a dark t-shirt and sucking his thumb. His blue eyes locked with mine and I let the kid inside. In the dark, I could make out he was around five or six and completely scared out of his mind."Shh. You have to be quiet." I hid behind the door, putting myself in between him and the danger outside. I heard a lot of yelling and swearing from the front of the store and covered his ears.At the moment, we were safe.There was more crashing and I heard the clicking of guns being loaded before I crouched and covered the little boy's head and neck. It seemed to go on forever, the sounds being drawn out by the adrenaline and cortisol pulsing through my system. I swear I wasn't a praying sort of person until that moment.Whoever is up there, please protect my mom. Mom, please be ok. Please be ok.

After it had been quiet for a moment, I peeked under the door when there was a terrible stench wafting in. There was a sound; footsteps and they sounded close by. I covered my mouth and nose to keep from gagging. It smelled like sulfur and trash, like boiled eggs left in a dumpster for a week mixed with something else......dirt, maybe? Whoever was walking closer really had a dire need of fifty showers. I don't think I even breathed for a few seconds."I can smell you." The person outside said quietly like the villain from a horror movie. I didn't move a muscle.

Where were the cops?

As soon as the person crept just outside the door, I made up my mind: If the door opened, I would run as fast as I could to draw this shooter away from this kid. The figure stopped and I saw their shadow reaching under the door like a taloned hand. The door shook as they tried to pull it open and I saw something through the crack. A tail, an honest-to-God tail, draped on the ground.

I've lost it, now. I'm about to die and I'm hallucinating.

I waited for the door to creak open or for my heart to stop beating when the shaking stopped. The door latch turned and the door swung open, blocking my view. Something walked in, a staggering, brutish female shape. She looked around while making a snorting sound and, to my horror, I realized that she was sniffing. I didn't see much from behind the door, but I was able to see about half of the mirror.

If I hadn't lost my sanity then, I'd have lost it instantly at what I saw reflected back at me.

Oh. it looked like a lady, alright. A lady with one solid metal leg and the other covered in fur, topped with a cloven hoof like a goat or a donkey. What I could see of her face looked no better. She was a pale, stone-like structure and her red eyes glowed in the mirror, enough to convince me that I would need intensive therapy for seeing her face alone. I recognized her as the woman from the freezer aisle and saw that her nose was crooked and leaking black liquid from my punch earlier."Come out, come out, wherever you are." If she looked into the mirror or behind the door, we were dead. Satisfied no one was in sight, she walked out, metal leg clanking away. I silently picked the kid up and ran out of the room, certain she couldn't chase after me very quickly with the whole mismatching deal going on. I heard a growl then, I felt something clothesline my ankles and send me tumbling to the ground.

Dammit, the tail.

I twisted to protect the kid by falling on my back. The thing grinned, showing an impressive set of pointed vampire fangs in place of regular teeth."Ah, perfect. I knew you were close, little demigod. And you brought me a little appetizer, too. How thoughtful." I got up to my feet and looked her in the glowing eye. A long, thin tongue darted out and licked her lips, making the most horrifying slurping noise I had ever heard.Ugh, that is nasty.

"Look, I don't know what kinda sick game of hide and seek you think this is, but I'm not playing." I said, getting up and making sure the kid was hidden in the clothes rack I had put him in. If I could keep her attention off of him, I could probably get away. I remembered when my shirt fell back down over my back that I had a trick up my sleeve, too. Well, in my waistband, to be more accurate. There was silence in the rest of the store, so I was willing to bet everyone was already out or hiding. The monster looked at me sideways, flicking the light switch with her tail and stunning me with bright, white light.

"Well, don't you look tasty?" She took a step forward. "Go on and run if you want. I like it better when my food is scared. It tenderizes the meat quite nicely." She said, coming closer. "Hitting me was not a good idea, Cora." I felt my blood run cold at realizing that she knew my name. Not letting that stop me, I pulled the pistol out. Before she could react, I aimed for center mass with my shaking hands and pulled the trigger. The bullet lodged in her animal leg and she went down, hissing."I said no." I said as I backed up more and ran into the back of another clothes' rack with my ears ringing. I'm pretty sure that all shooting her did was make her mad because the She-Hulk got back up and screeched at me, her eyes glowing brighter with rage and her hands growing talons from the nails.

"That was very annoying. Now, I guess I'll have to make your death last longer." She lunged toward me and I dodged, sending her leaping into a clearance rack and me back to the floor. The gun went flying into a pile of folded men's jeans. She got back up and started barreling toward me. I got up and ran into the home section to hide. After grabbing a knife from a nearby display, I wedged myself into a shelf display of curtain racks. I was determined to die fighting and far away from the kid.

"There you are." I heard her voice hiss as she turned into the aisle I was hiding in, her animal and metal legs clunking in a mismatched rhythm on the linoleum. I tightened my hand over the knife hilt when I heard her running closer and braced myself to slash, stab, scream or anything else I had to do. The teeth didn't come and neither did any claws. There was a sick squelching sound, a scream and then..... nothing.

She exploded in a shower of green dust and I saw a guy holding a bronze sword standing where she had been seconds ago. He was tall with dark hair and bright blue eyes, the green grime settling over his orange t-shirt. I kept my knife up and I could see it shaking pitifully in my grip.

"Are you ok?" He helped me out from the shelf, checking me over. I nodded, shocked and turned when I heard something move, only to see the little boy standing by the start of the aisle. "DADDY!" He ran over, tackling his father's leg in a hug while hiding behind his jeans. "There was a monster. This nice lady helped me.""Did she, now?" He turned back towards me and I gulped at seeing that his bronze sword was gleaming with the same goo from his shirt. "Wait, you could see that thing?" He asked me while gently nudging my knifepoint away from him."

Um....yes. And I've got questions. What was it? Where did it go? Are you going to try to kill me, too?" All the words tumbled out as I dropped the knife, horrified."No, I'm not here to hurt you. I was just looking for him." He put a pen cap on the swordpoint and it shrank before my eyes into a pen, which he put into his pocket. "Sorry about the scare. I'm Percy." He offered me a dirty hand. In shock, I took it. "I'm Cora."

"Nice to meet you. Maybe you should come with me before more come looking. These things travel in packs, you know." Stunned, I looked around. The people were back in the swing of things like nothing had happened.

"I'll go grab my phone, first." I turned to go find it and stumbled. I needed a nap. I seriously needed a nap. My limbs felt heavy and my vision blurred a little, tilting to the left like I was on a rollercoaster.

"Easy. Let's go find a spot to sit down." He put the little boy into a nearby grocery cart and waved for me to follow him. He seemed to know what was happening, so I did.

Chapter 2

When we finally found a bench in the shoe department of the store, Percy sat down first, patting the spot next to him.

"Thanks for helping Charlie, by the way. He has a tendency to run from me in the store." The little boy squirmed in his father's lap. Seeing them together, I was starting to catch the resemblance. They shared the same blue eyes, dimples in their cheeks and the same curls in their dark black hair.

I settled next to them. "What was that thing and what did it want?"

He took a deep breath like he was getting ready to drop some heavy truth bombs on me. "That was a monster called an empousa. It's from Greek mythology. They're kinda like shapeshifting vampires. They like to hunt demigods." He mentioned it very nonchalantly.

Monster. Empousa. Greek mythology. Shapeshifting vampires. Demigods.

That thing had called me that word. None of this was making any sense. This seemed like something that Homeland Security or the FBI would know about.

"I'm sorry, demigods?" I asked, taking the galaxy fidget spinner out of my pocket to focus my restless energy.

"Yeah. Half human, half god. Before you say anything, you should know I'm one of them." He let that sink in and continued when I didn't respond. "The fact that you could see it makes me think you might be like us." He looked at my hands. "You have ADHD? I'm willing to bet you're dyslexic, too?"

My breath hitched in my chest. I had been so careful to not tell anyone I knew because I thought it was embarrassing. So, how could this stranger that I've known for five minutes pinpoint my learning disabilities that quickly?

"Most of us are. My dad is kinda a big deal, so it must have smelled me or Charlie. Here, take this." He passed a business card over to me and I accepted. In bold, black print, the words read

'Delphi Strawberry Service, Long Island, NY.' There were also some letters in white ink, but I could read them fine.

"Camp Half Blood." I turned the card over and saw a picture of a Greek temple, like the kind that you would see in a historical movie. It had columns and a huge open structure, all built in alabaster white.

"That was written in ancient Greek, not English. You're really proving my point, here. If you don't mind my asking, are either of your parents out of the picture?"

This snapped my attention back to the present.

"They just got divorced, actually. Look, I should really be getting back to my mom. She'll be crazy worried about me." I started getting up, certain that this had been an elaborate prank. He nodded, grinning a little bit.

"Alright. My number is right there if you change your mind."

I glanced at it again and there it was, scrawled untidily in blue-inked pen.

"Wait, that wasn't there before-" I looked back up and the man and his young son were gone. I was left alone, thinking I had just imagined the whole thing.

"Cora, there you are! I've been looking everywhere for you." I felt a hand on my shoulder and flinched. It was my mother, looking concerned as she brushed my messy hair out of my eyes. "Oh, honey, you look like you've seen a ghost. Let's get you home." Her pastel pink nails caught in the light and she led me back to the freezer section.

"I might as well have." I murmured.

Percy looked around the busy parking lot of the apartments, waiting to catch sight of the silver Taurus when his cell phone rang.

"Seaweed brain," His wife, Annabeth, started when he picked up. "You said you would be back an hour ago. Where are you?" He smiled a little.

"Well, Wise-Girl, were you worried about me? I just got held up, is all. I think....I think we may have found a new half-blood. Can you tell Chiron to send a satyr?" Percy's Spidey Sense was tingling like crazy about this girl. Not only could she see the empousa, she had tried to fight it with no training.

After a pause, Annabeth's voice returned. "I'll let him know. What about that nest of draconae we keep hearing about?"

"I took care of it. And the emposai. We'll be there soon, I promise." He passed the phone back to Charlie. "Mommy wants to talk to you."

Charlie squealed and took it into his eager hands, leaving Percy to continue scanning the road for the girl's car.

"Now, we wait."

I came out of my room to help my mom set the table for dinner. After quietly watching her for a minute, I decided that it was a good time to bring up what had been bothering me.

"So, Mama? I think we may need to update my sleep meds. I'm getting weird dreams again." I had insomnia that could lead to horrible nightmares and days at a time when I would get no sleep. That could cause hallucinations, which would explain what happened earlier. About two years ago, Doctor Grant had put me on a child's dose of Restorii, but I was 17 at this point so maybe it was time to get something stronger.

She paused while putting the final touch of parmesan on her pizza slice. "I think that we should wait until we are absolutely sure it's the meds. It could be stress-related. Have you been tense about shool or your dad?"

I hesitated. My father and I hadn't really been close and he had hardly ever been around. He ran a small trucking company and was always off making deliveries or supervising some corporate event. The fact that he had moved out with his secretary had been rough for me initially, but I hadn't really been stressed by it. What bothered me most is that it had hurt my mother badly. We had come home from a day out together to find him packing his bags. My mom had told me to go wait in my room and I had. Behind that shut door, I heard my father tell her that he wanted a divorce and he had found someone else. I heard my mother calmly ask if he wanted to tell me and he said that his new girlfriend didn't want to have a stuck-up teenager in the house. That is when he left and my mom had started crying.

I had thought that I never wanted to see my mother cry again, so I had tried my best to be the perfect daughter. Good grades, keeping my head down and staying out of trouble. I don't know if today counted as legitimate or not, so I didn't bring it up.

"No, no more than normal. But, I think I am hallucinating again." I went to grab the pitcher of lemonade from the fridge. "I saw a monster in the store, today." She dropped the pizza cutter onto the stove with a loud clang.

"Oh, that must have been while I was in the bank. There was a little commotion in the front, though. Maybe that's what you saw." She smiled at me, her brunette pixie cut catching in the sunset's light. I paused again, confused as to why she was referring to an attempted robbery with gunshots as a 'little commotion.' I knew I should probably explain more about what happened, about how I hallucinated shooting a monster in the clothes section. I remembered about how my hands had been shaking and my ears ringing for at least twenty minutes after the blast. But, how exactly do you approach that subject: "hey, Mom, I think I shot somebody in the store today. Well, actually it was a monster trying to kill me?" It was probably best for everyone to just forget about the whole thing.

"Yeah. Maybe it was the mean old lady wanting to use her six-year-old coupons for thirty pounds of cat food again." I added, laughing a little to ease the tension.

My mom set my plate on the table, ruffling my hair. "I'll call the doctor in the morning." She paused at seeing something on the counter. It was the business card I had left there. "Hm, I wonder what this is." She picked it up and examined it with her librarian's steely focus.

"Um…Hunter at school gave it to me. Said it was a promotional thing for a job he's taking." I faltered. I couldn't do it. I didn't want to upset the delicate balance we had right then. Things were finally back to normal.

Dinner proceeded this way for the rest of the night. We watched bad reruns of Glee, got ready for bed and I started prepacking her lunch for work tomorrow. I heard her on the phone with my aunt through her cracked bedroom door. She talked to my Aunt Ronnie a lot, especially lately.

"I just miss him, you know? I keep expecting him to just walk in and say 'Hey, beautiful. What did I miss?'" She was talking about my father again. I set her lunch bag in the fridge and grabbed the laundry basket to start folding clothes, pondering what that strange man had told me in the store.

There was no way that guy was telling the truth. Gods? Monsters? The only monsters I had to worry about were local politicians and the ACT coming up. It would best to just forget about the whole thing, but my mind kept revisiting the event without my permission. I looked at my hands, the ghost of that pistol going off in my hands fading like an old picture. That had felt very real, but there's no way I had actually shot that gun. I didn't have the training or the resolve to do such a thing. I was lost in these thoughts when my mother's voice caught my attention again.

"I think it was my fault. I drove him out." I kept working and her voice lowered a bit. "No, he didn't want anything to do with her. Said that that girl didn't want a teenager around." she paused, listening to her sister's response. "No, I don't know if he knows.

He's never around her long enough." They were probably talking about me and how Dad doesn't know what my opinion is on the matter. I picked up the basket to put the clothes away when I heard something that made my stomach plummet through the floor.

"She isn't his, that much is true." There was a pause with a loud warbling on the phone that told me Aunt Ronnie was talking loudly. "Well, it's pretty obvious, Rachel. She looks nothing like him and he was never around. It's not like we were exclusive at the time, anyway. Plus, she's way smarter than him." She paused and I heard her bed creak like she had sat down on it. "No, she doesn't know. It's best that way."

My skin went cold. I couldn't swallow or breathe. I heard my heartbeat roar in my ears as my eyesight started rimming with black. Everything froze around me. It was so quiet that you probably could have heard the bugs chirping outside. I quietly set the basket down in the hallway and went to the kitchen. I was yanking my hoodie on and writing a note on our chalkboard at the same time.

"Went out for a walk. I'll be back soon."

I left quietly, locked the door and flew down the stairs. I needed space and the night air helped me think.

If my Dad was not my father, I had a growing suspicion that what that crazy guy in the store had told me wasn't that crazy after all.

Chapter 3

Annabeth had told Percy when he got the phone back that there was already a Searcher assigned to her and to sit tight. Apparently, they had already been planning an extraction mission for a girl that matched Cora's description for a while. After learning this, Percy had been about to drive off back to the hotel when he caught a glimpse of her running out of her apartment. She was running like she was being chased. He put the truck back into gear and followed slowly, just to make sure she was ok.

Nothing was pursuing her but she looked very afraid and bolted to the courtyard next to an old playground. He watched as she sat on a swing and put her head in her hands. He glanced back at the car seat and saw that Charlie was asleep, his curls resting against the window. He cut the ignition and the lights to avoid drawing attention as he watched.

I ran directly to my favorite swing on the playground. As I sat and let myself think, I started to feel so angry and confused.

If my dad wasn't my father, who was? More importantly, what was I supposed to call him? I couldn't just call him Shawn, as that felt too weird. I thought back to when I was a child, to the very few memories I had with him there. Him pushing me on this swing, him taking me out for donuts on my birthday, him laughing at a dumb joke I had told him about tornadoes. I looked back on all of these and felt out of place, a fraud.

Man, I need therapy.

"Penny for your thoughts?" A voice said. I looked up and it was my friend Alex. She was usually out this time of night and took the swing next to mine. She must have just gotten off of work because she was still wearing her uniform from the Ulta down the street. I don't know when this girl slept because she was always either at school or at work. Her blood must have been pure caffeine to stay awake as long as she did.

"It would take a whole lot more than just a penny." I stared at my hands.

"Well, what's wrong? I've got time." She smiled, the little chip in her front tooth glinting in the light. We had been friends for a while and she knew a little about the situation with my dad (not dad?) leaving. It felt wrong to not fill her in.

"Turns out, I have reached Disney princess status." I started swinging my legs.

"How so?" She swung as well, her long and lean frame looking slightly awkward in this swing that was built for children.

"Ready for some drama?" I paused long enough for her to nod. "My dad left two months ago? He is not my biological father. I heard my mom say it on the phone just now." She was silent at this fact. I looked up at the full moon surrounded by stars for guidance. "My mom has been lying to me."

"I......I don't know what to say. Other than I'm sorry." Alex never really talked about her life at home, so I assumed it was worse than mine.

"So, what's new with you? What big adventures are you planning on going on?" I asked her, desperate to get off the subject.

"Nothing much. Just the ACT coming up soon." We both groaned in unison at the mention of the ACT. The one test that would determine the course of our college lives was scheduled to occur in a few weeks just before summer break.

"Think you'll do ok?" I asked, eternally nervous about tests.

"I hope so, I'm planning to do a blood sacrifice to the moon tomorrow for luck." I laughed when she said this. Dark humor usually did me a world of good when I was sad. She started skidding to a stop, her brown hair taking almost a full 2 seconds to catch up to her.

"It's the science that I am worried about. I just know there will be at least one section on physics and you know I suck at that." I blinked in surprise, relieved that she had confided in me.

"I'm worried about the math. The numbers with letters give me a headache." I took a deep breath, smelling the sage bush and the sand. "If you get a good score, where will you go?"

"Probably TSU. I'll get a good scholarship there and they have a great food science program. How about you?" She dug in her pocket and offered me a Jolly Rancher.

"I honestly don't know. I'll probably stay here and take care of my mom. Maybe go for teaching or something." I took it, unwrapping the green candy and putting it in my mouth.

"You'd be good at that. But, if you could go anywhere, where would you go?" She was always asking me these things and I never really knew an answer that pleased her. Her light brown eyes looked at me, baring into my soul for an honest answer.

"Uh, probably.......I might like to do video game coding or animation. Maybe in California or New York?" It was a pipe dream, sure, but that seemed to satisfy her curiosity. She was quiet for a moment and I stopped swinging.

"Is something wrong, my dude?"

"No, it's just....We have so much we can do. I just don't want to disappoint anyone."

I snorted a little.

"You? Disappointing anyone? Nah, dude. You're Mrs. Perfect. If anyone is disappointed by anything you do, that's on them. You get straight A's, you're president of the Dungeons and Dragons club and you volunteer in the library. Any school would be lucky to have you." Never let it be said that I wasn't supportive of my friends. Alex deserved a good pep talk every now and again. She smiled at me again.

"Tell you what; after the ACT is over, no matter how it goes, you and I go get a victory pizza?"

I sighed, getting up.

"You know that 'pizza' is one of my favorite words. But, my mom doesn't like me going out." I glanced at the time on my phone.

10:15 already?!

"Time for me to go. Goodnight." I started walking home.

Alex watched her go. She licked her lips and tried to imagine the taste of Cora's flesh as she would sink her fangs into her neck, her small arms flailing around as they slowly stopped moving and the fear dimming her blue eyes.

Soon.

Alex looked up, catching a whiff of something else hanging in the air, something much stronger than Cora's scent.

"Hm.....Another half-blood. Awesome, I'll get two snacks in one night." She smiled and started following the smell. It smelled salty and Alex tried not to drool with excitement. She was starving and the fact that a demigod was so close, one of the children of the Big Three no less, was driving her crazy with desire. In the back of her mind, she thought that she should be careful. Her sister had gone hunting at the store earlier that day and had not returned. But, eventually, the hunger won out against her better judgment and she began following the trail. She was so hungry that she threw caution to the wind by walking straight up to the blue Toyota Tacoma truck that was waiting in the parking lot. She sniffed around and sensed some movement behind her before a sword sliced its way through her abdomen.

She didn't even have time to scream before she turned to dust.

I heard a loud noise when I was walking home that sent me jogging back to the staircase. When I got back to the building, the outside lights were all out. Mom wasn't in her usual reading chair on the balcony. I smelled the salt tang of blood before I even got to the stairs. I ran up, two at a time. My apartment door was hanging off of its top hinge, the 306 sign next to it smeared with red.

"Mom?" I peeked inside, getting my phone out to call for help.

The apartment was a disaster. I stepped inside and looked at the overturned furniture, the dirt and glass all over the floor. Church was hiding under the couch and hissed when I tried to reach for him. I heard something moving around and craned my head around the corner to look in the hallway.

"Mama?" I tried again, afraid of what might be happening. I heard a solid thud and crept along the wall to my mother's room.

Robbery. It had to be. I must have just walked into it. I reached into my pocket to call the cops, but I remembered that I had left my phone in the laundry room. When I glanced through the crack in my mother's door, I froze. There was a giant form hovering over her on the floor, her cell phone still in her hand. There was blood at her hairline and her arm was bent at a weird angle, but she was breathing with her eyes shut. The thing standing over her turned and it was......nightmare fuel. Nightmare fuel for sure. It towered around two feet or so over me and was built out of snakes. Where legs and arms should have been, it had two snake trunks. Its face.....Oh, god, its face..... two horrible, yellow-slitted eyes jutted from a serpent's skull and a long, forked tongue was darting out every now and again.

"I jussst wanted to know where ssssshe was, woman. I wasss going to let you live." It turned and faced me, the pupils in its yellow eyes slitting. "Ohhhh, there you are. How nicccccccce of you to join ussssss. I wasssss jusssst talking with your mother. Ssssshe sssmellss ssssso good, but you..." Its tongue flicked out in my direction and it sighed. "You will make a better meal." Its voice was like walking through leaves, hissing and falling in a very sick imitation of a human voice.

"L...Leave her alone." I glanced around for anything I could use as a weapon and came up with a wooden piece of the couch arm. I raised it in front of me. "Leave us both alone and...and I won't hurt you."

It hissed and it took me a minute to realize that this thing was laughing. "Issss that sssssooo? Well, my ssssssissssstersssss are coming over assss well. I wouldn't want them to be hungry, now would I? And demigodsssss jusssssst tassste the bessssst." It moved toward me with lightning-fast speed and I jumped out of the way as its fangs snapped at the spot where my head just was, lodging into the doorframe as I shut the door in its face. I backed up as the door was yanked back open and I swung the stick in front of me, lopping off its tongue on the next lunge. It made an ear-splitting high-pitched squeal and I got an idea. If I could just lead it to the open balcony window, I could play Chicken with it off the third-floor ledge and get it out of here.

I just had to distract it.

"You want a snack? Eat this, Lizard Legs!" I threw a broken chair at it and it sidestepped easily. That's when I heard another loud hissing behind me while a mass of fur ran by my feet, climbed up its body and started viciously attacking its face.

Church.

It shrieked again and whipped its head side to side, sending poor Church directly into the wall. He got up and ran off to hide again. It charged after me and I saw for a brief second that the eyes were now clouded and bleeding profusely. My cat had blinded the thing.

Good boy.

I waited and ducked, stabbing my makeshift spear into its back and kicking it over the balcony railing. It screamed on its way down and landed in a pile of snake trunks, still on the sidewalk. After I caught my breath, I ran back to check on my mom. She was knocked out cold, the blood oozing from the back of her head. I started trying to wake her up by gently hitting her cheek.

"Mom, wake up. Come on, it's Cora. You've got to wake up. Someone trashed our apartment." I got up to go get some water when I heard some strange shuffling sounds coming from outside. I went to inspect it when I noticed the monster was gone from the sidewalk. The thuds were coming up the stairs.

Oh, no. The fall didn't kill it.

I grabbed the nearest object, a broken broom from the ground, and waited at the busted door. When it was slowly pushed open with a menacing creak, I swung as hard as I could.

"Woah, woah, woah. It's ok. Easy." A human hand caught my broom, blocking it from hitting his very human head. "See? Not a monster." It took me a minute, but I recognized him and lowered the broom. "What happened in here?" Percy asked, keeping his hands in front of him as if he was calming a rogue dog.

When I caught my breath, I answered, "I don't know. There was this thing, it busted up my place, it hurt my mom and I pushed it over the railing." He nodded and went to check out the scene. I stood frozen at the doorway, wondering just how much the neighbors had heard. He came back into the living room, careful to avoid the glass shards littering the floor.

"Your mom is fine, just a concussion." He started trying to clear a path. "We should bring her to the hospital on our way out."

"I'm sorry, out? Out where?" I raised my broom again. "I'm not going anywhere with you. Stay back." He eyed it like he was trying not to laugh and stepped closer. I backed up and he stopped, putting his hands in his pockets and eyeing me carefully.

"Three monster attacks in one day says otherwise. I know a safe place to take you, but now they know where you live. The safest thing you can do is come with me." He took another step and I stepped back, keeping the distance between us.

"Three?" All the energy started draining from my limbs, making everything heavy. "Wait, earlier, in the store..."

"It was real."

"Then how were there three? There was the one just now and that one vampire in the store. That's two." My head was spinning in pain and confusion.

"There was just another one outside. I took care of it. Here, sit down. I'll tell you everything in the truck, but we've gotta go before more show up." He settled me down on a cleaner part of the floor and went back to get my mom. He carried her downstairs and came back for me.

"Are you hurt?" He asked and I shook my head. "Can you walk?" My voice wasn't working and I stood. He helped me down the stairs and into his truck. The little boy from earlier was asleep in a carseat in the back, next to where my mom was buckled. I looked back at my apartment and bit my lip nervously.

I had a bad gut feeling that it was the last time I would see it for a while.

Chapter 4

He glanced at the kid in his shotgun seat and wondered if this would be considered kidnapping.

"Put your seatbelt on." He reminded her. In her shocked state, she must have forgotten. She looked at him, eyes unfocused.

"Why? I thought you couldn't die in dreams." She clicked it into place and he backed the truck out of the space and put it into drive.

"Now, can you tell me what did this to your mom?" He started driving to the nearest hospital.

She hesitated. "You're not going to believe this, but it was a giant snake with legs."

Another draconae. Good, at least her short-term memory is functioning.

"I believe you. Those are called draconae. I'm surprised that one managed to get up there, though. They usually don't climb stairs." He was trying to chatter to make her feel better. Her mother moaned in the backseat.

"You said earlier in the store that I'm like you. What does that mean?" She cut right to the chase, done with his nonsense.

"Well, I am a demigod or a half-blood. My father is Poseidon, the god of the seas. I was actually here on a mission to break up a monster den when I saw what happened in the store." He turned onto the local highway. "So, any idea as to who your parent is?"

She stared out the window. "No. I just found out tonight that my dad is not my biological father. He hasn't been in the picture for a while, though."

He paused, letting her grieve for a minute or so while we made a turn. "So, it's one of the male gods, then. Let's see; blonde hair and blue eyes, smart, good fighting instincts. Could be Apollo or Hermes. Zeus hasn't had any kids in a while, and neither has Dionysus." She snapped her focus back to him.

"Eyes on the road!" She ordered. He looked back up and swerved into a turn he had almost missed. He didn't miss how she cradled her hand close, though.

"You should have told me that you got hurt." He turned into the hospital parking lot, searching for the Emergency Room entrance. "We can check it after we get your mom situated and then we have to go." He found a spot and started to park. "Stay here with Charlie."

"Are you kidding me? No, I'm going in with you." She unbuckled and jumped out to the cement. She opened the door and started getting her mother out. Percy saw something strange; the stubborn tilt of her clenched jaw reminded him of someone and he couldn't quite remember who. He helped her carry her mother inside while holding Charlie in his other arm.

The nurses at the desk dropped what they were doing and rushed over.

"There was a break-in and my mother got hurt." Cora explained quickly. They settled her into a chair while they waited for a gurney. Percy kept an eye open for any trouble. He sat down and looked at his phone.

1 new message

He opened it up and read.

Grover is coming down. Stay put! His ETA is in 20 minutes.

This calmed him down some. His best friend would help get her there safely and he could get back to his family vacation. Percy tapped his hands anxiously as they wheeled her mother out. The nurse on duty, Grace, handed Cora a clipboard to fill out. She grabbed a pen and started writing quickly, hands shaking slightly. Considering how this is probably her first day dealing with monsters, she is doing better than I did, he thought. After a while, Percy stood up as the doors opened again and Grover shuffled in. He was wearing his usual rasta cap with his usual fake shoes and jeans. He was wearing an old yellow Six Flags t-shirt with some suspicious food stains on the fabric. Grover walked over and Percy met him halfway.

"Hey. What are we dealing with, here?" He asked in a hushed voice. Hospitals made him nervous, too. Too many smells and injured people.

"I found that girl, Cora, in the store." Percy nodded to the girl pacing by the lobby chairs. "Since watching her today alone, there have been three monster attacks. She saved Charlie from one, even." Grover glanced in that direction, searching. "Her, the little one in the blue plaid jacket." He gestured with his thumb towards her. Grover looked over and took a deep breath, smelling. He frowned and nodded.

"She's a demigod, alright. I can smell it from here. Very powerful, I'm guessing by her scent. Any idea on her godly parent?" Grover kept watching her, narrowing his eyes in concentration.

"I think it is her father. She just found that out, though, so go easy on her." Percy watched her put the clipboard on the desk. She returned to the chair and tucked her jacket around the sleeping Charlie. Grover walked over and she looked up, tense and about to bolt like a startled animal.

"Hey, there. You must be Cora. I'm Grover, it's nice to meet you." He smiled, offering a hand.

"This is a friend of mine. He can help you." Percy started picking Charlie up to go, passing her jacket back to her.

"Hi." She responded, taking her jacket back. Percy left the two of them alone in the lobby to talk.

Well, things just went from bad to worse.

My stomach was in knots by the time they wheeled my mother back. I debated going back with her when the nurse told me I couldn't because I was a minor. Right at the moment, I was fiddling nervously with my lava rock and gemstone bracelet. There was no one else in the waiting room, so Grover and I spoke quietly.

"So, you're also under the impression that my biological dad is some Olympian god?" I asked, not entirely wanting the answer.

"Yes. And now that you know, more monsters will come after you. You aren't safe out here. There is a place we can bring you where you can train." My pulse started roaring in my ears at hearing this.

"Sorry, train for what, exactly?" My mouth felt like cotton.

"To fight them and keep yourself alive. It isn't safe for half-bloods out in the open mortal world. You can get hurt by both monsters and mortal weapons." He looked into my eyes, trying to convince me. His brown irises had little flecks of gold in them and I tore myself away.

This guy was telling me the truth.

My mind was reeling with all of this new information. This was not a decision I wanted to make. How could I possibly leave my mom? She had done everything for me, given up who knows how much to keep me safe and they all wanted me to just leave her alone in a hospital? What would she think? She would go out of her mind with worry. Then, I thought of seeing her broken form on that gurney and the memory made me want to hurl.

I had caused that. She had gotten hurt because of me.

"Will..." I struggled to form the words. "Will Mom be safer if I go?" I searched his face, hoping for a sudden laugh, him to say 'just kidding!' and walk away. I had no such luck.

"Yes, she is mortal. They will leave her alone." He glanced out of the sliding glass doors. "We have to hurry. Do you have a getaway bag or anything? We probably shouldn't go back to your house. It'll be swarmed with police and monsters." He got up, offering a hand to me. I took it, finding that I stood exactly as tall as him.

"No, I don't. How will we get there?" I asked, following him.

"Turn right outside the door." I followed his order and saw a small gold car parked a few spaces away from the entrance with a Ferrari emblem on the hood.

"That gold car is yours?" I asked and he grinned a little.

"Look harder." He responded, keeping pace with me. I looked back and the light bent strangely around the vehicle. When I blinked the light out of my eyes, there stood two winged horses lashed to a chariot. In the chariot stood another blonde girl around 20. She looked me dead in the eye with her stormy, grey irises almost glowing in the night's darkness.

"Wait, wasn't that a car a second ago?" I asked.

"No, it just looked like one. That was the Mist playing tricks on your eyes. It keeps the mortals from seeing our world for what it is, but it can mess with demigods sometimes, too. The chariot was always there." He explained as the girl narrowed her eyes at our approach, taking in my old jacket, my grey camo shirt, jeans, and boots.

"This is her, then? I'd have thought you'd be more....impressive." She stated in a disappointed tone. I set my jaw as Grover clambered in behind her, offering me a hand.

"And I thought that chariots went out of style centuries ago. I guess we're both disappointed." I took it and followed him into the deathbox. There was a little handrail, but not much else to stop someone from falling out of the back.

"Annabeth, don't be rude," Grover said as he took hold of the railing next to me.

"What? You and Percy wake me up at midnight on my vacation and ask me to be the designated driver and don't bring any coffee or anything? Sorry that I'm cranky." She glanced back at me. "You might want to hold on."

I grabbed onto the railing. "Are there seat belts on this thing?"

Grover laughed as Annabeth took the reins and got us moving. After a moment, the horses unfurled their wings and I realized what was happening.

"Wait, are you going to FLY us somewhere?!"

"Of course. It's the fastest way to Long Island." Annabeth smiled as the chariot's wheels left the ground and I screamed "Do you even have a pilot's license?!" Once I realized that we were, in fact, not going to plummet to our deaths, I opened my eyes and looked down, seeing that we were in the clouds. We were at airplane cruising altitude with cities zipping by faster than I'd even thought possible.

"So, what's your name, kid?" Annabeth yelled over the roaring wind.

"How are we not dying?!!!" I was freaking out.

"The pegasi are well-trained. What is your name?" She asked again, steering.

"C....Cora."

"Nice to meet you, 'C....Cora.' We're going to land at Camp in a couple of minutes. Just sit back, relax, and thank you for flying with Chariot Airlines." I turned to Grover, who, honestly, looked quite bored.

"Camp? How are we going to fly to Long Island in a few minutes? That's a 3-hour plane ride."

"The simple answer is magic. The long answer is that these pegasi are fast and the Mist protects us from being seen. As long as we don't run into trouble, I think we will be there soon." Annabeth answered in an I-know-more-than-you-do tone. I saw a flash of light off to our right and realized that it was lightning. Grover looked closer.

"Annabeth?"

"I see them. Hold on tight!" She swerved and the chariot lurched in the opposite direction when something hit us in the side.

"Cora, get down!" Grover shoved my head down and I felt something stir a few pieces of my hair.

"What is it now?" I asked, getting more scared by the minute.

"Here, put these on. No matter what you hear or see, keep your head down and hold on." He put some noise-canceling headphones over my ears and took the reins from Annabeth. She turned around and drew a long, white sword. Through the wind burning my cheeks and blowing my hair around, I made out a distinct horse shape galloping towards the back of the chariot. As I watched, Annabeth swung her sword and there was a horrible screech as it disappeared. It continued like this for a few more moments when I glanced up and saw that we were heading downwards toward a sandy beach.

I saw Grover turn to tell me something and the chariot jolted. My hands came loose and I flew out of the back of the chariot directly into the freezing water 20 feet below.

Chapter 5

R io de Medici had just been awoken by a nightmare, the same one that he had woken to the previous night. He tossed around restlessly while he tried to go back to sleep and forget about it. He was facing the window and dim light was bleeding through to his eyes. He reached over to pull the curtain shut when he noticed movement over the Lake. He was glancing out of his window when his eyes settled on the chariot. He brushed back the blue curtains to see it clearer. The Camp chariot was being pulled by two pegasi and coming in too hot toward the Lake. Annabeth Chase was in the back and it looked like Grover the satyr was steering the reins. Another person with long, bright hair fell out of the back and tumbled into the water.

This made him get up from his bunk to go to find his shoes, trying not to wake his little brother, Austin, up. He tugged on his white windbreaker as he ran outside quietly to see if he could assist.

They needed help alright. The pegasi were thrashing and making an awful mess with the reins while Annabeth and Grover tried to get them loose. The third person was nowhere in sight. He rubbed the sleep from his eyes and called out to them.

"Hey, do you need help?!" He went to ring the warning bell by the boathouse. After giving it several rings, he kicked off his shoes to wade in, going to help calm the horses. Annabeth was soaked and had an impressive cut on her cheek from the crash that caught in the dim lighting when she turned to see him.

"Rio! Yes, desperately. We need to get everyone to shore." She was looking for Grover, who was still over by the deeper end of the water and searching frantically.

"Alright, I can help with the horses. Can you get the chariot un-stuck?" He went around and gently calmed the first one enough to start untying him.

"Yeah." She went to work hacking at the weeds trapping the wheel. "Grover, come give me a hand."

"Annabeth, she fell in." He came over, touching her arm.

"Yes, we all did, Grover. The horses are going to get hurt if we can't get them loose." She waved a few more sleepy helpers over from the shore.

"No, I mean that she hasn't come up, yet!" Grover said louder and finally got her attention. Rio understood that Grover couldn't swim on account of not having human feet.

"Wait, there's someone under the water?" Rio asked as he looked up to where Grover was pointing. Before he knew it, he had released one of the horses and swam over. Taking a deep breath of air, he dove down and looked around. In the darkness, he couldn't make anything out past a few spooked naiads. He surfaced and sloshed back over to higher ground in a hurry.

"I cant see. Anyone have a light?!" He called. One of his brothers, Will, came over. "I can try." He said, taking off his wet shirt and diving with Rio under the water. The glow from Will's skin helped significantly and Rio was able to see all the way to the bottom. A naiad came close and gestured wildly for them to follow her. He swam in her direction and she pointed to a girl floating motionless in the water with her leg completely straight like it was anchored. Rio hurried over and saw why; she was tangled by some underwater plants by her ankle. Will dove to cut it with his pocket knife while Rio went to get air.

"Hey, we found her!" He called and waved for help, but it didn't look like anyone heard him. He took a huge gulp of air and dove back down. Will passed him and Rio could see that she was still stuck.

She probably hasn't breathed for almost three minutes.

He glanced back at the weeds and saw it was too clumped and thick to cut through quickly. This girl needed help and she needed it fast. He whistled as loud as he could underwater and a few of the naiads wandered over with sharp shells and went to work on it. Aware that they were pressed for time, he put himself at her level to check for any obvious injuries. The naiads cut through the weeds and Will grabbed one of her arms while Rio hauled the other. They brought her to the surface just as one of the small motorboats was passing. Zoey Channery was at the wheel and her brother, Connor Stoll, looked at them.

"He's got her. Help push her in." She said, watching Connor gently take her by the armpits while Rio and Will pushed. The combined effort had the half-dead girl in the boat in seconds, followed by Will and Rio. Will looked at her and checked for a pulse in her neck.

'She's still not breathing, but I've got a heartbeat. We need to start CPR." He started on chest compressions while Zoey started the motor back up and Connor took the helm. As Rio watched, she didn't respond. Will did two more rounds before calling for a switch and Rio took over. Rio was starting to lose hope when he started on his second round.

"Come on, come on. Breathe." He said, silently begging any gods that were listening to help them. The boat was pulled onto the beach and he laughed in relief when he heard a sound: a hacking cough.

"She's awake!" He helped her get on her side and beat his fist on her back to help her cough the water out. Will jumped out to talk to Annabeth and Grover when the girl finally looked at Rio with startlingly blue eyes. In the dark, Rio could tell her wet hair was very light, probably blonde, and that her skin was very pale white. That would explain the gold blur he had seen. She looked very scared when she saw him and started struggling to get away.

"Easy, dolcezza. I won't hurt you." He helped the girl sit up. She calmed down and he helped her take off her soaked blue and black plaid jacket to replace it with his own. "Here, that's better, right? What possessed you to go chariot-diving in the middle of the night?" The girl nodded blankly and Rio saw blood starting to trickle down her temple. Connor whistled quietly and Zoey smacked him in the shoulder as people started flocking around.

"I fell." She said hoarsely, giving him a steely glare. Rio heard footsteps and looked up as Chiron walked up to the boat.

"Well, that was quite the entrance you made." He looked at her and smiled. "Bring her to the infirmary, Mr. Solace. I suspect she has need of it. Thank you, everyone, but it is time to get back to bed." Will nodded and walked back to them, putting his shirt back on.

"Hi, there. I'm Will. Can you walk, yet?" The girl tried to balance on her feet and staggered. Rio caught her and swept her legs into one arm, supporting her torso with the other while stepping out of the boat. "It's ok; I've got you." He started following Will and Chiron to the Big House. She hardly weighed anything to him and he had no trouble carrying her across the strawberry fields. He could feel the sharp angles of her ribs and shoulder blades as he held her shivering form. She looked around strangely at everything as if bewildered by the camp setup.

"What's your name?" Rio asked, trying to get her to feel better.

"Cora." She responded, eyes rounding back to him.

"Ah, a beautiful name for a beautiful girl." He smiled, trying to make the situation better and she frowned at this effort. "My name is Rio. You fell out of the chariot. Do you know what happened after?"

"Not really. I hit something when I fell in the water." She touched her forehead and Rio could see more bright red blood gathering at her hairline. He set her on one of the infirmary cots and stepped back as Will checked her vitals.

"You must be the new kid that Hunter went to find." Will said and she nodded.

"I know a Hunter." She responded in a flat tone. Will was checking on her irises with a penlight when Chiron and Rio watched, their stupor only broken when Annabeth and Grover walked up.

"Grover, I think you might wish to tell me your report now." Chiron started. Grover nodded and launched into a story about how Percy had called Annabeth and Annabeth had called him in the middle of the night about this girl that was a demigod being attacked by local monsters while Will stepped out for her to change out of her wet things. Chiron listened intently, but Rio's focus was on this girl in the cot once the curtain was opened again. She let Will check her head and wrist, which looked like it had been previously broken or sprained. Now that her color was coming back, he could see she had a light bronze tan and a strange bracelet on her wrist. She looked at him again and sized him up by looking him up and down. She wrinkled her nose a little in distaste.

Rio grinned a little. "Like what you see?" He flirted. She was rather cute wet and covered in mud, which meant that she was probably exquisite when dry and clean. Plus he loved it when girls smiled or giggled at his compliments. There had to be something wrong with this one, though, because she didn't.

"I just wanted to say thank you." She was talking to him and Will, hardly even smiling. This struck Rio as strange because he and his brother were both very easy on the eyes and girls ogled them both constantly. He wasn't used to being dismissed. Rio had always laughed when ladies got annoyed at figuring out that Will was in a relationship with Nico di Angelo. "Oh, well, more for me." He always joked.

Will bandaged her wrist and muttered under his breath when he inspected her forehead. Getting an ambrosia square and a canteen of nectar from the cabinet, he offered them to her.

"I think you could have a concussion. Try taking these and they should help." Rio noticed that Grover, Annabeth and Chiron had halted their conversation and were watching with apt interest. Cora took them and eyed them warily.

She just figured out she's a half-blood he realized.

"Here, you eat this one and drink the other. Do it slowly." Will suggested and she did so. The room watched with bated breath to see how her body would react. After a moment, the bump on her forehead stopped bleeding and began to close, prompting a long sigh of relief from the audience.

"There we go, good as new. How do you feel?" Will asked, sitting on her infirmary cot.

"Like I can outrun a train." She tightened and released the fist of her injured wrist. "What was that stuff?"

"It's called ambrosia and nectar. They are the food and drink of Olympus and they can heal demigods. Try not to take much more than that or it can burn you up." Rio smiled a little as Cora's eyes widened and she pushed them away.

"Alright, I think you can walk now. Chiron, it's your turn to talk to her. I'm going back to bed." Will left, followed by Anna-beth and Grover. Rio followed them, glancing back to make sure everything was ok. When he was convinced, he walked back to the Apollo cabin while lost in his thoughts.

Clearly, it was his hero complex talking, but this little girl refused to get out of his head. He kept picturing how pale and lifeless she had looked under the water with her blonde hair floating around her head. He wondered what would have happened if they hadn't found her and this sent a bolt of sadness through him. Frowning, he shook himself loose.

Get a hold of yourself. Let her be someone else's problem, now.

I woke up to someone pounding on my chest. My eyes flew open to focus on this boy with close-cropped dark blonde hair and hazel green eyes performing CPR on me. I opened my mouth to ask what happened and a whole chestful of water burning through my mouth and nostrils silenced me. After they brought me shivering and soaked to the infirmary, I found myself wrapped in this warm blanket nest and squinting at the bright light. My head hurt like someone was using a jackhammer inside it and my left wrist had long since gone numb.

Not as numb as I felt, though.

I was so worried about my mother lying in the hospital bed alone. She might have been awake at this point and wondering why her only child had abandoned her. I felt a pang of guilt when I thought about it. She would be so upset and confused, not to mention scared.

Good, let her be scared. The evil little gremlin part of my brain thought, making me feel worse.

"Let's start at the beginning, shall we?" I looked up, having almost forgotten that this guy was still there.

The medicine had helped a little with the pain, but I had a feeling I was still in a little bit of shock. He looked like he was in charge by wearing a simple white buttoned shirt and black slacks that were both crisscrossed with wrinkles as if he had dressed in a hurry. He had long dark hair drawn back into a short ponytail with a short, dignified matching beard that framed his studious brown eyes. It was then that I realized he was in a wheelchair. Professor X stared at me like a guidance counselor looking for answers and I sat up straighter, trying to gather some form of discipline. The man continued speaking.

"I am called Chiron and I run this Camp. What is your name, child?" He had a slight accent that made his words flow strangely to my ears. Not quite British, but similar.

Dangit, I need a new nickname for him. Professor X won't work.

"I'm Cora, sir. Cora Locke." My throat was still sore and it sounded raspy. He reached over to the minifridge and retrieved a cold box of apple juice, handing it to me.

"Here, you might feel better if you drink something." He paused for me to insert the straw and take a sip. "What all do you know about this place, Cora?"

I thought carefully about my answer. "This is Camp Half-Blood. A place for demigods, the children of the gods and mortals, to be safe from monsters. And train to fight them. Did I get that right?"

He nodded, impressed. "Yes, you are correct. And you just took ambrosia and nectar without burning up, so that proves you are one. How did you find out about all of this?" His eyes searched mine, gently probing for information.

"I was attacked in the store earlier. There was a guy named Percy there who killed the monster. I could see him and everything else fine. He told me what was happening and to call him if something else happened." My voice caught on this sentence. "And it did. Tonight, they broke in and hurt my mom." I bit my lip nervously.

Chiron nodded solemnly. "You're very lucky. Not many newly discovered demigods can survive two monster attacks in one day with no training. I am extremely sorry that happened to your mother." He put his hand over mine. "You must be exhausted from the journey here. I only have a few more questions and then I will see to getting you a place to sleep." I nodded, feeling comforted by the old gentleman's action. "Now, how old are you?"

"I'm 17, sir. Just turned 17 in April." He looked very surprised when I said this. I knew that I was small for my age, but not enough to warrant that expression.

"17? Usually, you are discovered or claimed by your godly parent by 13. Have you been claimed by anyone? Think back. It would have been something like a strange, glowing symbol over your head." I thought back to when I was that age.

"No, sir. Nothing comes to mind." Chiron knitted his eyebrows in confusion.

"What about any special skills? That can usually help narrow down the list of possibilities." Saying that made him kinda sound like someone giving a job interview.

"I'm good at sports like horseback riding, archery, track, soccer, volleyball. I like to read and write. I'm not that great at most other things though." I listed the bare minimum because I was getting very tired. He nodded and stroked his beard, perplexed.

"Well, we have time to figure that out. What about any strange abilities or likes?" He asked, cocking his head a little to the side.

"Other than liking things like science fiction, anime and my weird thing for peanut butter on Oreos, I can't think of any. Sorry." He nodded and backed his chair up, gesturing for me to follow him.

"We'll get you into bed and we can talk more in the morning. Things will look better after you rest." I got up and wobbled a little on my legs before getting my balance. I reached to grab my soaked jacket and held it close. He reached behind a desk in the corner and brought out a simple black drawstring bag. "You can stay in the Hermes cabin until we know otherwise. They always have extra space." I nodded, accepting the bag and peeking inside while following him. There was a folded-up orange t-shirt, a pair of black cargo shorts, a few pairs of socks, toiletries and an official map of the Camp. I set the white jacket hanging on the porch railing of the Cabin pointed out as the Hermes. While rifling through things in the bag, we waited at the door. There was a symbol of the staff with two snakes twirled around it above it with the number 11. Chiron knocked on the door and one of the boys from the boat answered it.

"Hello, Connor. This is Cora Locke and she needs a bunk for the night." He turned to me. "Go on. They won't bite you." Connor smiled at me, gesturing for me to stay quiet and stepping aside to let me in. I hesitated and followed him inside. It was a typical summer camp cabin with bunks along the walls, sleeping boys on the left and sleeping girls on the right.

"Hey, there. Let's see; you can take the bed down here, third bunk on the bottom by the window." He stage-whispered. I nodded and tiptoed over, setting my bag down and racking my brain to remember who Hermes was. The Greek god of messengers and thieves, I thought. Maybe I wouldn't leave my stuff unattended.

"Bathroom is that door there. We have breakfast out in the common area at 7:30. Just don't cause any trouble and you should be fine." Connor smiled again. "Glad to see you're better. Goodnight, Cora." He wandered off back to his side of the cabin and I was left alone. I ducked into the bathroom and got ready for bed. I remember distinctly thinking that I didn't have my sleep meds and that I'd never fall asleep on my own with how wired I was. I was very shocked to find out that my body had other ideas. As soon as my head hit the pillow, the blackness crashed into me and pulled me under into a deep and dreamless sleep.

Chapter 6

Lights being turned on interrupted my sleep. I covered them with my pillow, groaning.

"Five more minutes." I grunted and heard a thud by my bed. I smelled Clorox wipes and glass cleaner before I realized that I heard some voices. They weren't my mother's telling me to get up for school. I didn't recognize them and I hoped that if I just didn't move, they would go away.

"Here she is!"

"She doesn't look that interesting."

"Oh, shut up. You think rocks are fun."

"Hey, rocks are great!"

"Should we wake her up?"

"I don't know, you do it."

"No, you. She may not be a morning person."

"Both of you, be quiet. I'll do it."

Apparently not.

I felt a hand shake my shoulder gently as I started rubbing the sleep from my eyes. Three girls were crowded around my bed and chattering like a bad infomercial with no skip button. The one closest to me had a dark brown undercut and a nose ring. She looked like the leader of the bunch. Her brown eyes were shadowed by acid-green eyeshadow and sparkly gold eyeliner. Her hand hovered a little over my shoulder as I sat up. She backed up a step, putting her hands in her jean pockets.

"Hi, good morning. I'm Jess, one of your counselors." I nodded and got to my feet as I started processing the universe again.

"Good morning, Jess." I responded, causing the girls behind her to titter with giggles. I was in the Hermes cabin at Camp Half-Blood. My biological father was still unknown and my mother was laid up in the hospital. Church was likely hiding in the wreckage of the apartment, if he hadn't already been carted off somewhere. "I'm Cora." The two girls standing behind her were eyeing me curiously like I was being displayed in a museum. She glanced back at them and gestured with her hand.

"This is Kaylee and Zoey. Don't mind them, they just live for new gossip." Zoey looked at me with her hazel eyes, twirling a strand of her long, auburn ponytail around her finger. She had freckles and stood about as tall as me with her bright blue Nikes on. It struck me that she was one of the girls who had helped me out of the Lake hours ago. Kaylee also had a splash of freckles across her nose and brown hair teased up into two buns on the top of her head. Her blue eyes narrowed as she looked me up and down. She must be the rude one I heard, I thought, making a mental note to watch my step around her. Her orange camp t-shirt was tied up, displaying about an inch or so of her hip bones over her jeans, including a little studded piercing on her belly button.

What was with all the piercings in this cabin? I myself only had the general one piercing on both my earlobes. Maybe there was a certified specialist in here or something.

"Breakfast is starting soon and we have to do cabin checks in a minute or so. Is this all of your stuff?" Jess asked me. I nodded, still a little shellshocked at the events of the previous night. "Well, we can visit the camp store on our way out. Maybe get you some more clothes or a hairbrush or something." She went on about to the other bunks to wake up more of the girls. Zoey sidled up to me and I caught the light scent of flowers hanging around her. Hibiscus or roses.

"Hi! Where are you from, Cora?" She asked. "I have the bunk right above you, so we might as well get to know each other a little."

"I'm from mid-Texas. How about you, Zoey?" I asked as I started trying to braid my sleep-tangled hair. Kaylee stayed off to the side, eyeing us every now and again.

"I'm from Savannah, Georgia." She glanced back at her friend. "Oh, don't mind her. She's just a little shy. Her bunk is next to mine and she hardly smiles. Poor thing's suffered a trauma, I think." She climbed up the side ladder to check on her bed's cleanliness. "So, they brought you in last night, huh?"

I started making my bed, folding down the covers neatly. "Yeah. Bit of an emergency and they had to bring me in quickly, I guess." We continued with this idle chatter for a few minutes while Jess and that boy Connor inspected the cabin. When they approved, it was a frenzy to get to the door to line up for breakfast. I had been to a few sleep-away camps in the past, so I knew this routine pretty well. We filed out and Zoey stayed by me.

"If you have any questions, you can ask the counselors. I'd love a reason to talk to Connor or Jess. They're both so nice." She smiled brightly at them. "Oh, that reminds me: most everyone in here has the same dad, so inner cabin crushes are off-limits." I glanced around, counting the number of kids in here. There were about 20 ranging in ages from 8 to about 23 that I could see immediately and I raised my eyebrow.

"I'll bet you're wondering why there are so many." She said.

Wow, she didn't miss a beat, did she?

"Well, the gods have a lot of time on their hands and Hermes isn't married. Plus, he is the patron god of travelers, so all the newbies get put in here. Out of all of us, I think only you and one other, Shawn, aren't claimed. He's that little guy in the front. I think he may be a Hermes kid, though." We walked out in two rows all the way to the common area.

"What about all the gods? I remember some of them are related. Are all these kids at Camp cousins to each other?" I asked, finally able to cut into the conversation.

"No, the gods don't have DNA. So, unless they're in your claimed cabin, they're fair game. Why? Do you already have your eye on anyone?" She poked me jokingly. I smiled a little bit, deciding that this girl was fun and that I liked her.

"No. I've never had the time nor the patience to deal with that."
We all sat at a long picnic table in front of place settings. All the
plates and cups were empty until someone sat in front of them. I
watched Zoey as she sat down next to me, said "Blueberry waffles
with orange juice, please" loudly and they simply appeared on her
plate. She grabbed her fork and knife. "Just tell it what you want."

I glanced at my own plate, thinking. "French toast with cinna-
mon and chocolate milk, please." The air above my plate stirred
and a little stack of the requested item appeared. It smelled exactly
like mine that I made at home and my eyes widened. I noticed
everyone getting up and scraping some of their breakfast to the
fire in the middle of the Common area.

"Offerings to the gods. They like feeling appreciated and freak out
when they aren't." Jess said on my other side. I hadn't even seen
her sit by me. I got up and followed her. I picked a little strawberry
from my plate and tossed it in.

Dad, I don't know who you are. I'm not even sure I believe in all
of this. But, if you could let me know that everything will work
out, I'll try to be nice.

I wandered back to my seat just as all the talking died down in
the room. All the tables fell silent as Chiron stood up from his
separate seat. He stood taller than any man I had ever seen and I

craned my neck to figure out why. I blinked a couple of times and I was convinced that I was crazy when Jess leaned over to whisper to me. "Yes, he is a centaur. Try not to stare." Under his waist was the lower half of a horse. I'm talking like brown legs, fur and hooves horse.

"Good morning, Campers. It is so good to see you all up in time for breakfast. I have a few announcements. First, all activity on the climbing wall will be canceled for today while it is being repaired." This elicited a groan from the tough-looking kids a few tables down. "Those are the Ares kids. Try to stay out of their way." Zoey whispered to me. I glanced over and realized why: the kids sitting at that table all had ripped clothes, jostled each other roughly and all looked like they were about to start a fight with someone they had not picked, yet. When they finally quieted, Chiron continued. "The main chariot is under repair as well for today. Nyssa, do you think you could be finished with that by this afternoon?" He looked at the table down the row from us with all the burly kids and one girl stood up with grease smears on her hands.

"You put way too little faith in us. We'll be done by lunch." Her whole table cheered and Chiron nodded his approval.

"Very good. Last thing: we have a new addition today. A few of you may have noticed the commotion last night by the Lake.

Everyone, please give a warm welcome to Cora Locke." I stood up when he said my name and waved shyly when everyone cheered. Even the Ares kids looked mildly interested. I sat back down and sensed eyes still on my back. I glanced around and saw a boy staring at me. The same boy from last night, Rio. He noticed me looking at him and winked at me before going back to his breakfast. I shuddered, cringing away from the open attention I was getting from him.

"Ooooh, now there is something juicy." Zoey had seen the whole interaction and grinned menacingly. "That boy is nothing but trouble."

I grabbed my fork and knife. "Meaning what?" I just wanted to ignore him. I had already thanked him for helping pull me out of the Lake and I figured that balanced the scales. That hadn't stopped my heart beating faster when he had picked me up last night. Or my face currently flushing at remembering how quickly he had started annoying me.

He was just being nice. Anyone else would have done the same in his position.

Zoey's voice brought me out of my mental fog. "He breaks a new heart every week. You're lucky because he doesn't normally go after the new girls."

"Well, good. I don't think I like him very much. He seems really fake." That's where I left the subject while I ate my food and observed my surroundings. Ares was the god of war and that fit with his kids. They were all arm-wrestling or having eating contests. They all had the same aura of throwing their weight around and being a little obnoxious. They all looked like trouble, so I made a mental note to give them their space.

The next group looked a lot calmer, all their kids having blonde hair and grey eyes while writing or playing with fidget toys. "Those are the Athena kids. Very smart, but like to be left alone usually." Jess pointed the groups out in turn to me. "Apollo, Hephaestus, Aphrodite, Demeter, Dionysus, Iris, Hypnos, Nike, Hebe, Tyche, and Hecate." I looked at the randomly scattered empty tables and found that Rio guy was sitting with the other Apollo kids.

Well, that tracks. I thought. He was currently talking and laughing with the other boy from the night before, Will. The sunlight caught a few strands of caramel highlights in his hair and the energy he carried with him smelled like money. I wrinkled my nose and changed the subject.

"Why are those tables empty?"

"Oh, those? Those are the Big Three, Zeus, Poseidon and Hades. The other ones are Hera and Artemis."

"Oh, the ones with no kids. Hera is Zeus's wife and Artemis never married." I remembered that from history class. "But why is no one at the Big Three tables?" Jess nodded.

"Very good. No one is there because those three made a solid oath to not have any more children during World War II. They were just too powerful. Although, Zeus and Poseidon both broke it. We thought Hades did, too, but his kids were born before the oath and he hid them in a sort of time hollow. But, as of right now, all three only have one living demigod child each."

"Oh, like Percy?" I remembered he had mentioned his father a few times.

"Yes, like him. Wait, how do you know that name?" She almost choked on her eggs.

"He's the one who found me yesterday." A few heads turned to look at me. Apparently, this guy was a big deal.

"Really? That's so cool. He's one of the most famous demigods right now. He came and found you?" Zoey said, looking at me expectantly.

"Yes. I was just in the store yesterday and there was a monster attack. He happened to be there with his son and came barreling in." This led to scattered mutterings of surprise and more heads turning to listen. Now, I was more than aware I had an audience, so I kept going.

"What type of monster was it?" Jess asked, fascinated.

"He said it was an empousa."

There were a few surprised gasps. A few kids looked at me in awe.

"An empousa was your first monster? Wow! Those are so scary and dangerous." Said the younger kid, Shawn, around a mouthful of Fruit Loops.

"Well, I had no clue what it was!" I laughed. "I just knew this huge, stinking thing was chasing me. So, I shot it. That didn't do anything and, the next thing I know, it just explodes in a shower of guts. Percy had shieshkabobbed the sucker into next week." They applauded quietly.

"Were you scared?" Zoey asked. "I know I was terrified of my first monster." I nodded.

"And then, last night, this giant snake thing came and broke into my apartment hours later. He was there, too, but I had already pushed it over the balcony." I laughed, thinking it was funny afterward.

"Yo, that's crazy! Was it a dragon or something?" Jess asked.

"No, it was a draconae. Wait, there are dragons, too?!" I responded in surprise. Everyone nodded and a few of them pointed across the Camp to the giant hill I saw.

"Yeah, we have one guarding the Fleece at Thalia's Tree." Zoey said.

"Wait, the Fleece? Like Jason and the Argonauts' Golden Fleece?!" Having a dragon was cool, but we were talking about the legendary cure-all.

Jess smiled and picked up her toast, spreading butter on it. "Yes. Percy and a few others brought it a few years ago. If you think that's cool, you'll freak out when you hear who our Director is."

I cleaned up my space as soon as I was finished eating. "Really? Who is it?" At this point, I thought nothing would surprise me.

Boy, was I wrong.

"It's Dionysus. He's not here right now because he is attending a Council meeting."

A god. We had a freaking god as our Camp leader.

She took my silence as funny and laughed. She and the rest of the table started cleaning up. "Let's see; our first lesson of the day is archery. Let's head out early and get the good targets, people!" I stood up to follow and suddenly realized that I felt like I really belonged here.

Chapter 7

I followed the rest of the Hermes kids to a miniature version of the Roman Colosseum. I hung back for a minute to admire the white marble gleaming in the morning sun and the architecture of the columns. I let out a low whistle of amazement and hurried inside as Jess and Connor were explaining our lesson. I saw that everyone else had taken seats in the stands already and found that girl, Kaylee, sitting by herself. I sat close by so that she would have her space and some company if she wanted it.

"Alright. So, we are all going to run some drills on firing at 20, 30 and then 40 yards just to see what we remember." Connor was already holding a beautiful recurve bow with polished brown wood. I looked at it and smiled, thinking it looked more like a musical instrument than a weapon.

"We'll divide into beginner and intermediate level groups and then teams of five to start and then we will combine and start the actual lesson. Beginners will go with me and intermediates will go with Jess. Good luck." Connor said, heading over to a section of straw targets. The kids around me started getting up and dispersing to their groups. I figured that it had been a while since I had used a bow, so I went with the beginner group to choose a bow from the peg wall. After glancing around, I found a dark green impact bow around my size. I picked it up and read the tag on the label.

50-pound draw weight, huh? Seems to be the best option for me.

After carrying it back to join the group, Connor counted us off into two teams of five. I was with two girls and two boys I didn't recognize, but I tried to smile in a friendly way. As we were selecting targets, another cabin group came in. I saw Connor look over and groan in distaste.

"Will, how many times do we have to have the same archery class as you? I thought Chiron had switched you with the Cabin Four kids."

The doctor from last night, Will, was a kid not much older than me. He was built long and lean with a dark beach tan and white strands in his gold hair. He looked like a male version of a Barbie doll. He came forward, assessing the situation of all of these Hermes kids cramping his style and frowning.

"He can't switch us until next week because Cabin Four's kids are busy planting the strawberry fields until Friday. Sorry. We can take the other side if you want." He offered me a small smile. Connor muttered how that was ok and the Apollo kids all migrated over to the unoccupied area of the arena.

I picked a target and Connor stayed by me to watch. The other kids had already begun readying their bows and I checked mine before nocking an arrow on the string and planting my feet firmly shoulder-width apart. I pulled it back and sited along the shaft to the target standing 20 yards away. I took a small breath and let it fly on the exhale. Less than a second later, I heard a solid thud and grinned. I had hit dead center on my first try. I reloaded to try again, the memories of summers past when I would go bow hunting with my cousins in San Antonio flooding back and guiding two more arrows home and into a tight grouping on the circle. I heard clapping behind me and looked at Connor.

"You might do better in the immediate level. Have you done archery before?" He asked as I started walking to retrieve them. "A few times, never anything serious." I yanked them out and trotted back to wait in line behind the 30-yard target.

"If you keep up like this, I might just send you to switch to a recurve." He grinned and the curls of his brown hair shaded his blue eyes in quite an elvish way. I shrugged, not wanting to be in the limelight more than absolutely necessary. He wandered on to check on someone else while I waited my turn for the next shot. I glanced around, totally bored while I waited. The inside of the building was decked out like in Gladiator with the low gates on the ground level, the stadium seats and the field that served as an arena. The kids in the intermediate class were running speed drills and doing pretty well. I looked around to observe the Cabin Seven group.

Man, these guys were masters. I watched one kid aim at the target and hit it in the center while wearing a blindfold. Another saw this and flexed by shooting backward, which I did not know was possible. The thing that caught my attention was a girl reloading a weapon that resembled a crossbow with multiple firing mechanisms on four sides. She loaded them all at once, fired, turned the contraption in her hand and would fire again. That looked like a fun toy that I wanted to try out.

The line moved and I realized it was my turn. Everyone behind me was staring in earnest. I loaded my arrow and let it fly. It hit in the innermost circle, this time. I smiled and fired again, hitting closer. My cockiness was at full throttle, now and I decided to aim for the small space in between the two previous arrows. I aimed carefully and let it fly.

It sank halfway in and directly in the middle of the target. Connor glanced over and gave me a thumbs up. I left my bow at the stand to go retrieve them when I saw a ball of orange light streaking toward me. In the next second, I felt like time had stopped. The flaming arrow seemed to slow down to a stop as I stopped thinking and sidestepped it. I blinked when it was over and the arrow hit the ground a few feet in front of me, flames still curling upwards. I retrieved my arrows, assuming everything was fine and that this was normal. When I returned with my arrows in hand, Connor was rushing toward me.

"Are you ok? That was almost a hit. How did you dodge it that fast?" I blinked and realized there was a small ring of people around the firing line that were all looking concerned.

"Yes, I'm fine. Guess I saw it just in time. Also, why is someone firing flaming arrows? It's not like we are training to invade Greece." I tried to play it off as a joke. My smile faltered when his stony face told me that it wasn't.

"Just be more careful. Did you see which way it came from?" I nodded, looking in the vague direction and seeing Kaylee standing there with an empty bow. I connected the dots and arrived at a strange conclusion: had Kaylee tried deliberately to shoot me?

No, it couldn't be like that. She might not have liked me, but that didn't mean that she would shoot a flaming arrow at my head.

Would she?

Connor rushed over to her and I proceeded to fly under the radar for a few more minutes. I went to get some water from the water fountain when I bumped into someone.

"Oh, excuse me." I tried to walk around when the boy turned around, showing a smiling face with familiar hazel eyes.

"Oh, no. It's entirely my fault. Here, you go on ahead, sweetheart." Rio grinned, stepping to the side.

Sweetheart? I listened for any hint of a southern accent and found none. Which meant one of two things; he just called everybody that or he was making fun of me. I did not like either outcome.

"Thanks?" I took the opportunity and stepped in front of him while keeping eye contact. "Hey, I don't really like that. Can you not call me that, please?"

He looked mildly surprised at the request.

"Sorry. Would 'love' work better for you?" He smiled, showing an array of perfectly white and straight teeth. I felt my ears heat up with irritation as I tore my gaze away. Looking up at him like that was starting to hurt my neck.

"No. I don't want a nickname." I went to get my water. This guy was getting on my nerves and I just wanted to get out of there as fast as possible.

"Well, in case you change your mind, you know where to find me, Goldilocks." I felt his smirk as he leered at me. I moved out of the way and stared him down.

"Is this fun for you, making new girls uncomfortable just for getting a drink?"

He grinned more and bent to get a drink from the fountain. When he straightened back up and wiped off his mouth, he said "Yes, actually. Especially the pretty ones."

I rolled my eyes and walked away. He followed me, grabbing at my shoulder. "I mean it. You are way too pretty to be alone. Why don't you come hang out with us?"

"No, thank you. And don't call me 'pretty.'" I shrugged him off, walking faster. "We have a class to get back to." He looked crestfallen and tried to slow me down again. I walked around him when he called out, "So, tonight, then?"

Without turning around, I asked, "What about it?"

"I pick you up at 8 and we go canoeing. I promise it will be fun. Unless you don't like fun, either." I glanced back and he had his arms crossed over his grey breastplate with a few boys flocking into a group behind him. One of them leaned forward and whispered something in his ear, causing him to smile and his blonde hair to catch the sunlight like a halo.

So, that's what this is about. He is trying to show off to his buddies by picking me up. I honestly felt a little objectified and felt my shoulders tense. I was getting a little mad.

"No, sorry. I've got something planned." I walked away quickly to the various sounds of shock his friends were making. I went all the way back to my bow and finally took a deep breath. Zoey had set up her bow next to me.

"Wow, you look hot. Do you need a break?" She asked, wiping sweat from her forehead. Even hot and sweaty, she was still a knockout with her cute freckles and red hair. I wondered if she was a model or something. I glanced back at Rio, who was walking away with his gaggle of goons. I thought Zoey is the type of girl to go after. He should ask her out and leave me alone.

"No. Just a bit tired, I guess. It's been a rough couple of days." I started to reload.

"I hear ya. Tell you what, why don't you come down to the Aphrodite cabin with me tonight? A few friends and I are going to be getting ready for the bonfire together."

"Wait, why together? Isn't a bonfire just to cook food?" I asked in confusion. She laughed.

"No, of course not. The bonfire is where we link up with the people we like, we sing songs, make s'mores, play games and so on. It's how we socialize." She fired an arrow, landing it in the second ring. "Dangit! Missed again."

"Try dropping your arms a little, relaxing them at the shoulder. It helps me to aim better." I loaded an arrow and took aim at the 40-yard target. She did so, adjusting herself to become a lethally honed weapon. If I could have frozen that image, I would have said she looked like a modern-day Artemis on the hunt. She let it fly and it hit in the center circle. We both cheered and an airhorn rang out. We looked to find Jess in the middle of the arena, can raised in the air.

"Good job everyone. We have finally arrived to the fun part. Who wants to try out the moving targets today?" A few kids raised their hands and she waved them over. "Now," she paused for effect. "I need everyone else to put on armor. We're going to play tag!"

I didn't know what that meant, but it resulted in mixed screams of joy and groans of outrage.

"Tag? What's so great about tag, Zoey?" I asked, putting my bow back into the wall like everyone else.

"Well, we do it differently. You'll want to get that set of armor on."
She pointed to the display next to it.

"Why?" I asked, highly suspicious at the way she said it.

"We are the targets.

Chapter 8

When Zoey told me that we were the targets, I laughed. Then, I quickly pieced together that she was, in fact, deadly serious because she wasn't laughing along. She helped me with my armor, as I had no idea how to put it together.

"The other team will have paintball-tipped rubber arrows. If they get a body shot on you, you're out. The object of the game is to get to their home base without getting hit." She secured the last tie into place before going to assemble her own set.

"That sounds easy enough." I put on a helmet with a blue plume on it, grunting because it was the smallest size and still too big for me.

"It is when you are the defensive team. We are the offense on the first round." She sounded like she had already given up.

"Why is that a bad thing?" I made sure my shoes were laced tightly.

"We always lose in the first five minutes. That is the main reason we keep trying to switch archery class schedules." I glanced out to the other team when she mentioned this. They were in considerably higher spirits than us, joking around while getting ready.

"That is going to change today." I said, resolving myself to what I was about to promise. "I'll help you win." She looked doubtful and a few people around us glanced up. "Gather round, children, I have an awesome idea to try."

Rio was still reeling with disbelief. Usually, when he put on the charm like that, he would get a good answer or at least a smile. This girl had flat out told him 'no' and he found that a little aggravating. Louis had even come up and placed a heavy bet on if she had said yes. Which explained why Louis was frowning at the moment as he forked over the 6 drachmas to Austin. Rio's brain felt like it was short-circuiting, like a crashing computer as he watched the other team prepare for the game.

What's her problem? She was really hostile when I was trying to talk to her. Maybe she's not worth it.

He glanced at her pulling her long, blonde braid up and into her helmet and talking to Zoey.

Never mind, she definitely is. But, she's not into me, so it's time to move on. What about Danny or Sam? They're both really cute, not to mention available.

The thought of going out with Danny or Sam again brought the memories of all the time on the beach with Sam along with all the time goofing off in craft class with Danny. He smiled when he remembered how they had both almost swooned over him as he sang The Joker at the bonfire a week ago. With his mother's curly dirty blonde hair and green hazel eyes, he knew as soon as he had had his growth spurt that he was hot. When Apollo had claimed him during music class when he was 13, he honestly had not been surprised. That caused his status to skyrocket, bringing in all these new friends and girls. His light Italian accent was like a magnet to them and once he sang to them, they acted bewitched.

"Rio, what's got you so rattled? Is this your first rejection or something?" Austin sauntered up to him breaking him free from his thoughts. At 16, Austin was only a few months younger than Rio and he was also a musician. His abilities were more tuned for playing his saxophone, though. Rio found that Austin was more or less his favorite sibling and they did everything together.

"No, not really. But I just find how blunt she was strange." He put his red plumed helmet on and tore his gaze away. Austin cocked his head thoughtfully to the side before responding.

"Maybe she doesn't like grand gestures. Come on, I need you to lace up my chest plate." Nodding, he followed Austin to his discarded pile of armor. He methodically tied the fastenings and tried to focus on the game ahead. Red versus blue in a game of paintball tag. This would be easy.

"You shouldn't worry so much about it. We've got winning to think about." Austin suggested, trying to distract him.

"Yeah, you're right. Winning is more important than a girl."

A few moments later, both teams assembled to their sides of the stadium while Connor Stoll went over the rules. Play in the stadium only, if you were hit/you were out, no dirty tricks, no maiming, body shots only and wait for the whistle before starting a new round. The blue team left the stands so that the reds could scatter around and into position. Rio found his favorite spot in the stands, protected by the spire that would conceal his presence. The whistle blew and the blue team came running in.

The first thing that Rio noticed was that they were not all entering at once and those that were inside were scattering with shields raised. There was a flood of red-tipped rubber arrows that descended upon them and the kids that were tagged automatically went to the jail section. Usually, the Hermes cabin would just all run in at once towards the wall with no rhyme or reason. The only obstacle was that they were all very fast runners and could dodge and/or outrun the arrows at times. This looked like a new tactic. Rio pulled his painted arrow back and fired at the taller plume in the middle, Kaylee. He missed and there was a great, roaring cheer as a tight knot of the rest of the kids thundered in quickly, covering their heads with shields and moving in sync.

A distraction?! He fumbled with his bow as they ran in hooting and hollering. As soon as he realized his mistake, he reloaded and aimed at the one that was leading the others in a zigzag pattern. The leader looked like they were having the time of their life by running straight toward the wall. Rio pulled back his arrow and they looked directly at him. The pair of intense blue eyes that connected with his robbed him of his breath and he felt his hand waver on the bowstring as Cora raised her hand and gave him a one-fingered salute as he fired. He saw her smile, raise her other hand and actually catch his arrow in the air.

She caught it. In mid-flight. Rio shook his surprise off and couldn't help getting angry. And, he was very annoyed to admit, a little impressed. He loaded up another one and swore when he saw her touch the wall, smirking at him and forcing him to find a new target.

Just who the bloody hell was she?

The rest of the game proceeded like this and a few of the red team threw down their weapons in confused disgust when Connor's whistle sounded the end of the game. The Hermes team had won for the first time in close to a year. Rio wandered over to Austin, who was rubbing his eyes in disbelief.

"What the hell was that?" Rio asked, his accent trickling through in his angered state.

"I have no clue. They actually had a plan this time. I've never seen anything like it. Did you see how they were moving?" They started to walk down the stairs to switch their bows for shields.

"I did. That was surprising, to say the least." The blue team was celebrating by cheering and jostling each other about, putting the leader up on Connor and Zoey's shoulders and knocking her helmet off in the process, letting that long blonde braid tumble free. Rio felt an annoying jumble of negative emotions rising in his throat and freezing all rational thoughts.

So, this is how it is going to be, munchkin. He thought Well, consider this gauntlet thrown.

We won

The thought kept going through my head, turning my brain elated with serotonin. I felt almost like I was running on an adrenaline high when I went to find my bow to hide in the stands. It had felt so good to see the archers fall for our trap so easily, even better when I had seen the arrow hurtling toward me. In that moment, time had slowed down again and I had grabbed the shaft. I looked down at it still in my hand and smiled at an awful idea.

A truly wonderful, awful idea.

I knocked it into my string after finding the perfect spot to hide up in the wall, in between the gate and the pillar. No one would see me there, I thought as I monkeyed my way up and found the best spot to put my feet to stabilize myself. I had just settled in when the whistle blew and I waited for my prey. The first wave of the red team came running and dodging the onslaught of blue-tipped arrows. I scanned them, waiting for the best opportunity to fire at my desired target. My fingers and feet were starting to cramp up with this precarious position I was holding myself in. I watched as six of the nine Apollo kids that had run in looked surprised as the arrows found their marks and wandered off to the jail spot.

I really like this game, I thought.

With the next wave, Rio ran in leading the charge. I grinned, pulling back my purple-stained arrow I fired and got him right in the chest, sending him sprawling to the ground. He stood up, looked around in confusion and sulked off to the jail while scratching his head. Riding this gleeful feeling, I took down the other two before stopping.

If they saw me, my hiding spot would be rendered useless.

After two more waves, the whistle blew and everyone came out of their hiding places. I clambered down and dropped the final 8 feet, tucking into a somersault on impact.

Huh, didn't know I could do that, either.

I jogged to join the group gathered by the stands. Connor and Jess were settling everyone down to discuss the scores. After a few minutes of this minimal chaos, Connor smiled brightly.

"Guys, gals and nonbinary pals, we have a tie. 18/18, well-done everybody!" A voice chimed in "Actually, it's 19-18, Connor. I got hit." I swiveled my head to see Rio raising his hand, pointing to the chest shot I gave him. "It was a repurposed arrow."

Connor's eyes widened. "Wow, that's a first. Hermes cabin wins!" There was a cheer and Zoey came up to clap me on the back. "Everyone, it is time to clean up and head to our next class." Everyone started putting everything away. The Apollo kids looked dejected and in a general state of confusion. They weren't used to losing, apparently.

Connor came over and helped me hang up my bow.

"After that, I am bumping you up to the intermediate class for sure. That was brilliant." I smiled under the praise. "How did you make that shot at Rio, anyway? I never even saw you in that round."

Oh, he was good.

"Well, you see that spot in the crack between the gate and the wall?" I pointed. He looked and his eyes widened. "That is where I was. I took the shot when he was running right towards it."

"Yo, that has to be the coolest thing I've ever seen a newbie do." He turned back to me and ruffled my hair. "I really hope you're not a Hermes kid."

I froze at hearing this and I felt the blood drain from my face. Did....Did he not want me in there? Had I done something wrong?

"Can I ask why?" My voice cracked a little from the conflicted feelings threatening to leak from my eyes.

"No, it's not that you're not cool or something. There's nothing wrong with you. I'm just saying it would be weird to like a sister." He helped me down from the stool and my breathing resumed.

"Oh, I get it. Well, you've only known me less than a day. That wouldn't really make sense." I gently tried to remind him. He shrugged, walking out with me. "I think it would. You just proved that you're smart. You're also funny and you're easy to talk to." I cleared my throat nervously as we approached the next class. It was at a stable and I heard horses in the pens. I smiled and got excited, peeking in quickly. There were horses, the ones with wings from before.

This was a flying lesson.

I clipped on a helmet while I wandered over to the biggest pen.

"Ooooooh. Look at you."

This pen was closed and the faded sign over it said 'Goliath.' I looked over and beheld the biggest horse I had ever seen. He was absolutely massive and burly like Angola horses, almost twice as tall as I was. He looked over at me and snorted, his pure brown eyes focusing on me as if to say Shrimp, what are you doing here?

"Hey, you don't want to mess with that one." I looked at the girl who spoke. She had dark brown hair cut to a medium length and pulled back into a ponytail and her green eyes struck me by surprise. "He can be very mean." She looked at him standing alone in his corner, his black wings dragging slightly on the ground. "I'm Miranda, the Demeter counselor. Come on, class is about to start." She tugged me by my hand and I glanced back at the dejected pegasus.

I'll come back for you.

The basics for pegasus riding were the same as regular horses. Because of the press for time, Miranda took me to the side and told me that us two were just going to be riding on the ground today. Which was fine by me, as I hadn't even ridden a normal horse in years. When it was time to choose our horses, I found myself wandering back to Goliath's stall and Miranda stopped me.

"Oh no. He isn't for beginners. You can get really hurt even going near him. He bucked the last kid off so hard that he ended up in the infirmary with a broken leg and concussion." She steered me gently away by my shoulder.

"But, why keep him, then? If no one can ride him." She nudged me to another stall with a friendlier horse, the sign on his door saying 'Blackjack.'

"It's safer here for him than in the wild. He was born in captivity, so he is used to domestication." She let Blackjack out of his pen and he unfurled his wings, stepping to me and shaking himself off. He was a beautiful black mount as well, although smaller and more the size for me. He nudged at Miranda's hand and she smiled before giving him a little slice of apple.

"I think he likes you. It's important to have a good bond with the horse you ride." She handed another one to me and let me feed it to him. He took it gently and she strapped his saddle on snugly while I introduced myself.

"Hi. I'm Cora. Is it ok if I ride you today?" I pet his neck while he chewed. Without waiting for an answer, Miranda led me to a stepstool and set me on his back. She led him out by the bridle and handed the reins to me.

"Try leading him around the paddock a few times." I nodded and gently kicked his side, getting used to his steps. As more and more riders trickled out and walked their horses around, Miranda finally emerged on her own brown mare. I stopped Blackjack in line with the others to listen.

"Good, let's get started-" Blackjack jerked forward from his position and I glanced down. There was nothing on the ground to scare him. I looked sideways and the girl next to me had her eyes set on Miranda while her horse went to snap at Blackjack again. I moved him a little away and went back to listening.

"-We are going to practice our normal riding. We will go over walk, trot, canter and gallop. A few of you can even try the jumps today if you're feeling up to it. If we are brave, we can go over some aerial maneuvers, today. For now, I just want everyone walking." Miranda seemed very stern and I worried how this class would go on if she was this sharp the whole time. Everyone started walking their horses in the circle. The previous girl kept leading her pegasus too close to Blackjack and making me nervous.

"Hey, excuse me, but your horse is trying to bite mine." I told the girl riding him. She finally looked at me and I saw she had her dark hair tied into a low bun under her helmet. She wrinkled her nose and looked at her horse.

"Biscuit just wants you out of the way. You're walking too slow." She said in kinda a snooty tone.

Ah, my first mean girl.

"Sorry. I can move out of the way." I smiled and moved Blackjack a little faster as I felt her settle in next to me. Alarmed that she was seriously popping my personal bubble, I watched as she brought her expensive-looking riding crop on my leg. "Ouch!"

"Oops." She smiled and I glared at her as I brought Blackjack into a canter to get away. She came up behind me again and her horse went for another bite to Blackjack's flank, causing him to speed up.

"Cora, control your horse." Miranda called, looking concerned.

"Trying to." I called over my shoulder as Blackjack squealed, starting to get faster. I pulled on the reins in vain as he started running at a full gallop.

"You have to jump." She started bringing her horse closer to me as Blackjack spread his wings. I started trying to move my legs free when I realized that my left ankle was tangled in the stirrup.

Uh oh.

"Miranda, I'm stuck!" I heard some yells of fear that were lost in the wind as Blackjack passed the other riders and the world started to blur. I tried to untangle my shoe as I realized I wasn't even feeling him gallop anymore. I screamed as he took off from the ground and I tightened my arms on him, squeezing my eyes shut. The beat of his wings stirred the air around me and I blinked my eyes open when I realized we were flying.

The trees were just below us and we weren't that high off the ground, but we were moving fast. I tried to steer him back to the paddock. Riding on the horse was much scarier than riding a chariot behind it. His wings were beating behind my head and we kept rising. He started rolling and I felt my legs getting sore from how hard I was gripping him. We went upside down and I felt the contents of my stomach threatening to make an encore appearance.

You are a long way from home, little bird.

I looked around, certain I had imagined the voice.

"Blackjack, was that you?" I asked and he just nickered as we started to turn back upright.

Come on, you know better than that.

I ignored it, trying desperately to control my horse.

"I'm not going to just go away, dear." I was sure I had heard it that time and looked around again. There was a lady with long dark hair dressed in a pale pink dress and a full smile flying in the clouds next to me.

"Oh, what the hell?!" I yelped, almost jostling myself sideways off the saddle. She giggled.

"Now, hold still. I'll untie you, but you have to trust me." She reached over and got me loose from the tangle.

"What.....Who are you?" I asked, very confused. I had seen a lot of strange things in the last few hours.

"I'm a cloud nymph. My name is Aurora." She looked serious. "I've been waiting for you for a while. I knew your father."

As I finally calmed down, I realized something important.

"I don't have a father." Blackjack was gliding back towards Camp and I saw Miranda atop her brown mare and flying towards us at breakneck speed.

"Yes, you do...Oh, I see." She smiled again. "You don't know, yet."

"I don't know what you're talking about. I don't know what?" She vanished into a puff of clouds and Miranda pulled up next to me.

"Are you ok?" She asked, checking on my ankle.

"Yes. How do I get down?!" I couldn't keep the fear or embarrassment from my voice. She nodded and stayed close.

"You're not in trouble, just follow me. I know that he got spooked." She led us back to the ground and I jumped off the horse, running to the fence and hauling myself over it.

"Cora, you can't just walk out of class-" The rest of Miranda's words were lost to the wind.

I was done with this. This was all too crazy for me. I wanted to go home. I threw my helmet to the ground and just kept running, not caring where I was going, just away. I finally reached the woods and slowed down. I stopped by a tree and caught my breath. It didn't look like anyone had followed me. I heard a crunching noise and turned around to face it.

"Miranda, I just need a minute-" I stepped back when I saw an ant the size of a small car close by, its pincers dripping with a hissing, smoking green liquid. My throat went dry and I realized that I had no weapons.

I was a sitting duck about to be eaten by a giant bug.

Chapter 9

Ellis saw a blur of bright gold hair dart past him while he was on guard duty. He had signaled to his guard partner, Toby from Hephaestus, that he was going to follow and set off quickly. This girl was fast, dodging roots and curves expertly like a deer. After a few minutes of full-on sprinting after her in full armor, she finally slowed down and took a breath. Ellis was about to ask her what the hell she was doing running around like that at 11 AM when he caught the look on her face.

She was very pissed off. He stopped about ten feet away on the ridge above and watched her as she stared angrily up at the sky. He knew that anguished look she gave. That was the same look he used to give everyone who got in his way. A look of pure rage and fear.

The new girl, he thought, recognizing her from breakfast. He had thought she looked a little nerdy and shy before, but he was almost afraid of her at the moment. He was about to break the silence and talk to her when he heard a scuffing sound. He looked over and saw a Myrmeke barreling right towards her.

They're attracted to shiny things, He thought vaguely before reality sank in. Ellis, they're attracted to shiny things and she probably is the brightest thing for miles!

The girl looked straight at it as it entered the clearing and Ellis was already moving. He dropped in between them and drew his bayonet sword, angling the glare off to the side. The Myrmeke followed the light and Ellis pushed the girl back towards Camp while it scurried away. He silently thanked his father that he had chosen the brown camo armor for guard duty when he turned around and grabbed her elbow.

"Why are you out here?" He growled. "It's not safe out here, especially without a weapon. You could have been killed." He grunted. He hated it when people had no regard for their own safety. She looked at him and narrowed her blue eyes.

"I just needed to be alone. I don't know why I ran this way. Sorry." She jerked her elbow out of his reach. "What was that thing?"

He had been expecting to be yelled at in a rough voice. He was shocked to find out that her voice was gentle and even. Once he calmed down, he checked to make sure the monster ant was not coming back.

"Come on, I'll take you back." He sheathed his sword. "That was a Myrmeke. Nasty things. They like to bring bright, shiny objects back to their nest." He started walking and she jogged to keep up. He was about a foot taller and looked about 70 pounds heavier. Even though she was short, she kept up with him well.

"There are more of them. And they just lurk around the woods?"

"Yeah. These woods are full of all kinds of monsters. You have to be a special kind of stupid if you run in here without any protection-" He caught himself from being rude. "I mean, you must have been really upset to run all this way." She stepped over a hole in the ground created during one of their many games of Capture the Flag.

"I am." Her hair had come loose from her braid and fell into her face.

"I can't promise I'll be much comfort, but I can try my best." He offered a small smile, pausing his walk and sticking his hand out. "I'm Ellis from the Ares cabin. Nice to meet you."

She hesitated and took it. He noticed her hand was very small and very decorated with bright red nail polish and a beaded bracelet.

"I'm Cora. Cora Locke." That's a Greek name for Persephone, he thought while she continued talking. "You're right; I'm a little wound up. Riding class was a little too dramatic. Wait, I thought that the Ares kids were...." She trailed off.

"Rough? Wild? The back of the bus kids?" He suggested, enjoying the little smile she gave him in return.

"For lack of a better description, yes. Sorry for the assumption." She resumed walking, skidding a little on an uneven rock.

"Careful." He caught her by the arm to right her position and started walking again. "You'd have to be the first to apologize to me for that, Cora."

"Really? I'd have thought that people here were nicer than assuming the worst on first impressions." He chuckled at hearing that.

"Anyone ever tell you that you might have too much faith in people?" He could see the path starting to even out.

"No. Maybe you just have too little."

Stricken by the thought, he brought her the rest of the way back to Camp in silence.

"Well, I'd better get back to my post. No more running around in the woods." She turned back to him and pouted jokingly.

"Aw, but what if I wanted to?" She asked, making him bite back a laugh at remembering that he had to be serious when in uniform.

"Then, I might just let the monsters get you this time." He turned to go, waving goodbye.

"No, you won't. You're too nice to do that." In the corner of his eye, he watched as she grinned a little.

"No, I'm not, sweetheart. I'm just a certified asshole." He kept walking, finding that he enjoyed teasing her.

"Certified JD impersonator, maybe. Not an asshole, though." He glanced back and saw her walking away with her hands in her pockets.

If there were still people like her around in the world, maybe this summer wouldn't entirely suck after all.

GI Joe let me walk the rest of the way back to Camp on my own. Now that I had run off some energy, I felt better. Still a little annoyed at what happened in class, but better. I did my best to shake off the residual feelings of anxiety and embarrassment while I approached the end of the forest. The high that I had been riding from archery class was very much gone and a slight feeling of dread had replaced it. I got back to the paddock by the stables and Miranda came trotting over on her mare.

"Hey, sorry. I just needed a minute." She stared seriously at me for a few seconds before opening the gate and letting me in.

"It's ok. Just try to tell me next time it happens. Blackjack is waiting over there for you." She pointed her gloved hand towards the left and I nodded. I kept close to the fence as I made my way over, raising an eyebrow at seeing a few girls in billowing white dresses hanging around by the trees. When I tried to get a better look, one of them stared back and waved. I waved back, perplexed.

"Those are dryads, a type of nature spirit." I flinched as I looked at Zoey, who had snuck up on me again. I jumped back into the saddle, looking back at the dryads. "They are terribly nosy and love to cause drama with the Campers. You'd probably be better staying away from them."

"Why do you stay stuff like that? I was literally just looking at them." I walked Blackjack alongside her horse.

"Well, they do. Just last week, the tall one turned a girl's hair into dandelion seeds for kissing Pollux in the Dionysus cabin. Apparently, he had been leading her on for months and she got crazy jealous." I blinked, shocked that I was trusted with such a trade secret. The rest of class continued on like that, with Zoey pointing everybody out to me to whisper her gossip.

My god, this girl knows everything about everybody. I thought. Zoey talked a lot and seemed to think every situation needed her opinion added to it. I didn't mind too much, but it was a lot of information to absorb. I had tuned her out for a few minutes while we were putting the horses away when she suddenly grabbed my arm.

"Hello? Earth to Cora? I just said that Danny was given a solid punishment." She seemed adamant that I know this.

"Oh, sorry. Who's Danny, again?" I unbuckled my helmet and hung it back up on the wall while she stomped her foot, annoyed that I hadn't paid attention.

"The girl who was chasing you. She's the daughter of Aphrodite and always pulling stuff like that. Someone really needs to teach her some manners." She followed me and put her helmet by mine. "That would really suck if you two ended up being sisters."

"Why would that suck? And there's no way I'm in there 'cause I know my father is the godly one." We followed the other Hermes kids to the next lesson, her keeping up with me while chattering at 200 miles an hour.

"Because 1. I would be stuck without a bunkmate again and 2. She would tear your head off. She's seeing that Rio kid and is very uh...." she was at a loss for words "I guess the best term is 'possessive.'"

"Ah, I see. Well, she can have him. I find him annoying." I smiled at the confused little choking sound she made.

"What?! No, he's so nice and sensitive. Not to mention hot and has the literal voice of an angel. And, gods, that accent." She fanned herself. " Are you blind or something?" I laughed and shook my head. "Or do you not like boys? I know plenty of ladies that would love to meet you if you are." She suggested, ever eager to either help or get juicy secrets.

"No, I'm not either of those things. If you're that into him, why don't you date him?" The group was walking towards the big farmhouse overlooking the property. I reminded myself that it was called the Big House and I wondered what class we could have in there.

"No, two type-A personalities like us would tear each other apart. Plus, he is a Scorpio and I'm a Gemini, which means that fate has already told us we cannot be an item." She sighed wistfully before continuing on, "And just because we aren't compatible does not mean I can't think he's pretty. What's your sign, anyway?" She asked as we went up the steps.

"Oh, I'm a Taurus. My birthday is in late April."

"Great! I love Tauruses. Y'all have the most chill vibes." We filed into the house and went down a hallway. I saw that guy from earlier, Will, standing at the front of a classroom next to a projector screen and I took a seat in the middle of the room. This was a First Aid and CPR class, which I was already good at.

Finally, something normal.

Until a girl poked her head in and spoke quietly to Will while her gaze settled on me. She was big and built like a pro wrestler with military-length brown hair tied up into a bun.

"Cora, Spinelli needs you outside." Will said, causing a few concealed giggles from the other kids in the room. I got up to follow her, already on edge from the laughter and whispers. She led me out, narrowing her eyes as she looked me up and down.

"Mom or dad, newbie?" She grunted in a noncommital way while leading me out of the Big House.

"Dad. I just found out." I saw the kids from Hermes all plastering their faces to the window to watch us and realized this could not be any good.

"Huh. I honestly would have thought you were an Athena kid." She turned back towards me suddenly, going to grab at my head. I dodged, ducking and using her motion to whirl behind her and push her to the ground. Two more girls came up from the side of the porch and grabbed my arms, lifting me up and sending my legs dangling in the empty air. Spinelli stood up, wiping dirt from her nose.

"That was a good try, freshmeat. It's not going to stop your initiation, though." The girls next to me smirked as they started running with me hanging uselessly between them like a piece of luggage.

Initiation. I had seen enough bad high school movies to know that this was not going to be pleasant. I tried to tug myself free, but these girls had my arms clasped in meaty hands that were made out of iron. They carried me into the bathroom and set me on my knees in front of a toilet. It absolutely reeked in there. I stared at the scummy water as Spinelli stepped up behind me and rolled up her sleeves.

They were going to give me a swirly.

"Oh, hell, naw!" I pulled hard to one side to knock them off balance and dove under the one girl on the right as the one on the left fell into her, dodging the next grab from Spinelli. I kicked the door shut and ran to the door only to find another girl standing guard.

"This one is slippery, Spinelli!" She made a grab for me and I jumped out of the way, sending her sprawling facefirst into the waiting sink. Free at last, I ran out and locked them all in. I smirked, waving at them through the window before running back to class. They all started staring at me in open shock. I settled back into my seat, trying to catch my breath.

"Dude, what happened?" Zoey asked in a whisper. I smiled.

"The Ares girls tried to give me a swirly, so I locked them in the bathroom." I responded and she laughed into her hand.

"Wait, really? Dude, that's hilarious. I wish I could have seen their faces."

The rest of class went off without a hitch. The only other note-worthy thing is that Will accidentally showed us a picture of ahem anatomically correct nude people. When he finally settled down the giggling and commentary, he explained why it was important that we know where the defibrillator pads go on everyone. Zoey nudged me jokingly.

"Now, I can definitely ask Mr. Dummy to dinner. He looks like he can keep a conversation going, if you know what I mean." She commented with a wink. We both concealed our laughter as Will wrapped class up. I went to talk to him, telling Zoey to go on without me."Hey, um, Will? Do you have a minute?" I waited for him to face me.

"Yes. What can I do for you, Cora?"

"Well, here's the problem: I kinda left my house in a hurry and didn't have time to grab my sleep medicine. I have insomnia and I was wondering how to get another prescription." I stared at the front of his desk nervously.

"You came to the right place. Have you ever been without them before?" He clasped his hands in front of him.

"No. If I don't take them, I get hallucinations and sometimes days without sleep."

"I'll see what I can do. Why don't you follow me and I can give you a checkup to write you another prescription?" He walked over, holding the door open for me. I followed him, answering all his questions about dosage, my regular doctor and what kind of medicine it was. For the second time in as many days, I sat on the infirmary cot and let him check my vitals. He muttered something under his breath and raised an eyebrow.

"Is something wrong?" I asked, getting nervous at his shift in demeanor.

"I just can't really find any sign of insomnia on you. When were you diagnosed?" He wrote something down on his clipboard notes.

"When I was 15. Last night was my first time without it." He nodded and set down the clipboard.

"Can I try something? It would be much faster than a MRI or a sleep test." He put on his gloves while watching me.

"Sure. What is it?"

"Just an Apollo kid thing. He is the god of healing and sometimes, his kids can sense when and if something is wrong. We make great doctors because of it." I nodded and he put his cold, gloved hands on the sides of my head while closing his eyes. I felt.....warm. Warm and tingly as something probed around inside my head like a virus scanner on a computer. He removed his hands, shaking his head.

"No trace of any sleep disorders. Half-bloods do routinely have trouble sleeping. That's how we can get warnings of danger and even messages, sometimes." He took off his gloves and threw them away while I hopped down.

"So we are like radio towers?" I toyed with the lava rock bracelet on my wrist.

"Yeah, in a way. Watch your sleeping and report back to me to-morrow." Armed with this new information, I saluted him and walked out. This hour was the Hermes cabin's free time, so I decided to look around and think about what I had just learned.

I did not have insomnia. If that was the case, why had my mom and the doctor insisted I take sleep medication?

I was lost in these confusing thoughts when a familiar redhead bumped into me.

"I see you're cozying up to Will, now. Girl, you have a definite problem." She looped her arm through mine.

"How so, Zoey? I just had to ask him something. Not everything is linked to debauchery."

"Well, I know that. " She lowered her voice, divulging yet another secret, "I was just referring to the fact that Will doesn't swing our way." She giggled and I cocked my head sideways in confusion.

"And that matters to you because....?" We were passing strawberry fields and I saw the dragon for the first time from our spot at the top of the hill.

"Well, he is 1. Taken. 2. Not into girls. If you catch my drift." She seemed to be avoiding the word gay. She swatted at something above my head. "You've got a bug flying around or something." Her eyes widened and she stepped back.

"What? Is it on my face or something?" I asked. She shook her head, speechlessly holding her mouth open. She pointed above my head. A few more kids looked up and gasped. I noticed that all of them had their faces bathed in a strange gold light.

"C-C-C-Cora, l-l-l-look up." Zoey said, falling to her knees. I gulped and glanced upwards. I saw an arrow being flown around a pair of wings and almost swore. I knew exactly who had those symbols. I had really hoped this wouldn't be happening, and certainly not this god. I didn't want to-no, I couldn't be- his kid. I had absolutely nothing in common with him. Chiron trotted up, his usual cheer in stark contrast to the serious fearful atmosphere.

"Good morning, everyone. What are we all looking at?" He looked over at me and his smile left his face like he had been slapped. "Ah, I see. It appears as though you are being claimed by your father, Cora." He looked back at everyone who, despite various stages of shock, were all going to their knees in reverence. "Children, this is a very rare thing that I have never even witnessed. Hail, Cora Locke, the daughter of Eros.

Chapter 10

Well, this got awkward fast.

As soon as I got nervous enough, I batted at the symbol in an effort to get it to go away.

"Shoo! That's enough, you made your point." It followed me around, glowing brighter as if to mock me. Chiron smiled again and everyone started resuming their business. I just stared at it in shock until it eventually lowered and the golden light settled around me, blowing my hair around and into my eyes. I tucked it back behind my ears and gasped at seeing the small, gold mark left on the inside of my wrist. It was a small pair of wings about the size of a dime. I tried to rub it off, desperate to be rid of the brand.

"Well, this is something very new." Someone was standing behind Chiron. It was a short, pudgy man with receding hair in a cheesy leopard print shirt with a reddish nose. I hadn't seen him before. Chiron looked back at him and then to me again.

"Mr. D., this is our newest addition, Cora Locke. Cora, this is Mr. D., the Camp director." I nodded politely, remembering my manners.

"It's nice to meet you, sir."

"Hmmph." He looked me up and down before shrugging and stating that "You're a scrawny little thing, but at least you're polite. Alright, Nora, it looks like you will be moving into Cabin #21. It would be best to get your stuff moved out there before the other Campers find out." He walked on, waving unceremoniously. Chiron sighed in disapproval.

"That is about the nicest greeting I've ever seen him give someone. You being claimed is certainly good news. Eros hasn't had any demigod children that I recall. You'll have the whole cabin to yourself. Follow me, I'll help you find it." He waved for me to follow. Zoey was still staring at me open-mouthed like a fish. I shrugged and muttered an apology while we passed by.

Damn. At least it's not Zeus.

This was not going to be easy. Eros was the god of...well, sex, for lack of a better word. I had about the same amount of sex appeal as a popsicle stick. How does Eros being my sperm donor explain the random speed and exit strategies of the last few days? More importantly, how did Eros end up with my mom, the most serious and straight-laced person I knew? How did the god of intercourse get with my mom, a librarian that enjoyed blazers? It just didn't add up.

Did she even know? I felt my heartbeat stall. More importantly, did Mom even know where I was? I felt like the worst daughter ever for forgetting and dug out my phone to call the hospital.

"I got to watch some of your archery class, earlier. You have some raw talent, Cora." Chiron said, interrupting my thoughts. "Leading everyone to victory that way was very impressive." He turned back toward me, saw the cell phone in my hand and shook his head. "We try not to use technology here. It attracts monsters." I put it back in my pocket.

"But, I need to let my mom know I am ok. We had to leave when she was unconscious in the hospital. She'll be worried sick." I stared at my hands, feeling like the wind had been knocked out of me. He touched my shoulder and I looked back up.

"I understand. Tell you what, I have a safe, emergency phone in the Big House for times like this. Let's get you moved into your cabin and we can go call her together." At this sliver of hope,

I nodded. We continued to walk and we stopped by the empty Cabin 11 to pick up my stuff. I grabbed my drawstring bag and put everything into it, feeling like I was abandoning everyone. In the short time I had been there, I felt like I was already getting attached. I shook my head to clear it and returned to Chiron's side. He led me to this smaller cabin on the other side of the field. It was built more like a cottage than the other ones, painted white with red and light pink trim. I wanted to turn around and head back to the Hermes cabin after seeing the place where Betty Crocker stored her Easy-Bake ovens.

"Since you are the only one in there, you are also going to be the acting counselor. That means you will be responsible for setting your own class schedule, clean checks and attending counselor meetings every month or as needed. There are some rules, though. We try to keep all the cabins safe. This means that, unless you are visiting for a specific reason, there will only be children who live there allowed in. Quiet time starts at 10 PM unless there is Capture the Flag or a bonfire, which pushes it back to 11." I went up the white steps and he handed me a small, old-fashioned silver key. I slid it into the lock, frowning at the white lace curtains over the door's window.

"How long will I be here, Chiron? I have school and my mom to get back to." The door opened and I stepped inside.

"That depends on how fast you can train. I am not comfortable sending you back into the Mortal world without knowing how to fight properly." He answered as I flicked on the light switch and we looked around the inside of the cabin. It was set up like a college dorm with one room containing about four black metal framed bunks lining the walls. Up in the front was a little common kind of area with a small ping pong table, a little game table with stacks of board games underneath situated next to a black and white-spotted bean bag sitting on a pale red rug next to a shelf full of-

"Books!" I ran over, throwing my bag onto a random bunk to inspect the low, black bookshelf. There were a few really good authors, here: Sarah J. Maas, Cassandra Clare, Jim Butcher and, taking up the entire middle shelf, all the collected works of Julia Quinn. I avoided that shelf and blew the dust off of the Clockwork Angel copy before hugging it to my chest. This one had been one of my favorites when I was growing up. My mom had read it to me and we listened to the audiobook in the car on vacation when I was twelve. Chiron chuckled and I looked back at him before getting back to my feet.

"Sorry, I just got a little excited. Are these all for me?" I gently set it back into its place, intending to dust in here before long.

"Yes. The cleaning Harpies and a few of the Campers put these in here. Said that they were the books that they did not want in their cabins." My face fell at hearing that. "I'll leave you to get settled in. Lunch is at 12:30." He let himself out and I looked around at this space that was meant to be mine. The walls were a generic off-white and the other side of the cabin had a little kitchenette complete with a black minifridge and a little table. There were two doors next to it and I wandered over to check them out. One led to a pink-painted bathroom with a glass-paneled shower, a sink with a hanging mirror and a regular toilet. The other door led to a huge empty closet for hanging clothes. Determined I would not need that, I walked back out to the main room. I picked the top bunk in the furthest corner from the door and set my stuff there.

"This can work. I can put my stuff here and I can stock that fridge with soda. Maybe I'll even tear out these curtains and put blackouts instead." My windows all faced the other cabins and I was pretty sure that this thin white lace would not deter a pervy teenage boy if they figured out a girl lived alone in here, so the curtain change was a necessity. For now, I fixed the problem by putting the extra blankets over them. Stricken by the sudden light change, I was disoriented for a moment while I climbed down. I started unpacking my few items and organizing them. That only took a few minutes and there was still a whole half hour before lunchtime. I grabbed a bandanna from the bag they had given me and went to work dusting the place clean. It looked like no one had been in here in quite a while, judging by the amount of dirt and dust that had built up.

I had just been putting the broom away when there was a knock at the door. I set down the cleaning rag and went to answer it. It was Zoey, leading a few of the girls from the Aphrodite cabin, including that girl from earlier, Danny.

"I'm sorry, Cora, they made me." She said as the other four chattered excitedly. Rules be damned, I moved to let them in.

"It's ok. Hi, everyone. Welcome." I smiled as they filed in and started squealing in delight.

"Oh my gods, Zoey! You didn't tell us how adorable she is!" One tall, blonde girl came up and inspected me by walking around in a circle and taking my chin to tilt my head from side to side. I was so surprised that I didn't know how to react and Malibu Barbie clapped her hands in joy.

"No, bad, Lacy. I honestly can't take you anywhere." Zoey blocked her hand when she tried to touch my hair. "Cora, this is Ella, Davina and you've already met Lacy and Danny. They heard that you were claimed and wanted to come say hello."

"Oh, your cabin is so cute!" Ella, the dark-haired girl with the perfect tan and shiny, blue nails said from the bookshelf.

"Thank you. I was just doing some cleaning up. It's nice to meet you all." I went to talk to Danny, who was inspecting the bathroom with no traceable emotion. "Hi. I think we may have got off on the wrong foot, earlier." She looked at me sideways and I continued, offering my hand. "My name is Cora. You're Danny, right?" I smiled my best, friendly smile and waited anxiously. Finally, she turned and took it, expressionless.

"Yes. Nice to formally meet you, hun. Sorry about earlier. I don't know why Biscuit acted that way." Her dark skin glinted in the yellowish light and I smiled wider.

This was progress.

"Water under the bridge. Let me show you around." I gave her a brief tour and kept an eye on her. Davina found my closet and poked her head in.

"Hey, why don't you have any clothes in here?" She called out.

"I just moved in and I didn't bring any." There was an audible gasp from all the girls who had invaded my space.

"What?! Girl, we gotta get you some clothes. There are a lot of extras in our place. What's your size?" Davina ran over and excitedly started looking me over.

"Women's sizes are an absolute joke, but I wear a size medium t-shirt." She laughed and her red lipstick caught my eye. All these girls were really well made up and I felt a little out of place in my messy hair and dusty clothes. We all looked up as there was a loud bell starting to ring outside.

"Lunchtime. We have free period next. Why don't you come visit us?" Lacy asked as we started leaving. I grinned and nodded, which caused a flood of giggles and I followed them to the pavilions.

"There isn't an Eros table, yet, so you can sit with us if you want." Ella suggested. She was built long and lean like a gymnast and I found myself mesmerized by her cheerleader energy.

"Yes, that sounds good to me." She sat me down right next to her and Zoey sat next to us on her neighboring bench. I smiled a little awkwardly at Jess as she gave me a strange look. Zoey leaned over and whispered to her, pointing at me. I watched Jess' eyes widen and she nodded, giving me a thumbs up. I glanced at the front table and there was a redheaded girl sitting with Chiron.

"Danny, who is that?" I nodded in her direction. Danny looked over.

"Oh, her? That is Rachel Dare, our Oracle." She stated simply as if that explained everything.

"What's an Oracle?" I asked, requesting mashed potatoes and roasted chicken for my lunch.

"An Oracle is someone who houses the Spirit of Delphi. She can give prophecies and have visions about things that are about to happen. You go to her if you want a Quest." Ella added on while Danny requested a strawberry salad for herself and got up.

"Oh, ok. What's a Quest?" I asked and Ella gasped in surprise.

"A Quest is where you go and do stuff outside of Camp with a team of two helpers. I've never been on one. But Danny has, haven't you, Danny?" Danny nodded, returning from giving the fire a sacrifice.

"Yeah. We went to get Mom's sacred doves from the pirate traders in Boston." She explained. Ella and I got up from the table to go give our offerings and I noticed Rachel Dare staring daggers at me. I smiled and waved awkwardly while scraping a bite of my food into the flames.

"So, have you chosen a weapon yet, Cora?" Ella asked, trying to rope me back into the conversation.

"No, not really. I'm really good with a bow." I suggested and she giggled. "What's so funny about that?"

"Nothing. Well, actually, the bow is your father's sacred weapon." She stated as she plucked an orange slice from her plate and tossed it into the flames. We headed back and saw someone standing next to our table. We settled back into our seats when he turned and I frowned, suddenly not hungry.

"I'm sorry to tell you this, but you are sitting at the wrong table, Goldilocks." Rio said, twirling a long-stemmed red rose in his hands. I glared in return and the talking around us quieted down.

"Actually, I believe that I have more of a reason to be here than you, Aeropostle knockoff. I got Claimed a little while ago." I sipped my lemonade and watched him eat his words.

"Then, why are you here specifically? You said it wasn't your mom, but this is the Aphrodite table." This caused some murmurings and more people craned their necks to watch.

"I was Claimed by Eros and there isn't a table for him. So, I'm sitting with some friends who invited me." I grinned, enjoying the little annoyed twitch he was getting in his eye.

"Yeah, we brought her over. Why are you here, anyway, Rio?" Ella asked, giving my hand a reassuring squeeze to let me know she was on my side. He put his hands in his pockets, trying his best to look bored.

"I came over to talk to Danny." She looked up at hearing this, apparently having been ignorant of the fact that he was standing right behind her.

"What about?" She asked and everyone leaned in to hear. He grinned and climbed up onto the empty table next to us. Everyone in the common area fell silent.

"This is for you, Danny. Austin, Kayla, hit it!" Blinding us with his smile, he started singing with the music they played their instruments from their table, the rest of the kids tapping out the beat on the wood. The song he played was an old one that I knew from a few movies called Can't Take My Eyes Off Of You. I hated to admit it, but he was a good singer. He went around singing on the tables and everyone cleared their lunches to give him room, cheering and singing along.

Completely surprised, I looked at Zoey who was humming along.

"I told you he could sing."

"When did we end up on an episode of Glee?" I asked to no one in particular as he started getting to the end. In total Heath Ledger style, he got to our table and led her up to stand with him. When the last note was over, Kayla launched a confetti cannon over them and everyone applauded. I tapped Ella's shoulder.

"Ella, is this normal here?"

"Yes. He does this kind of thing at least once a week. They have this cute little on again off again thing going on." She admitted, eyes set on them.

"That doesn't really seem like a healthy relationship." I stated and she laughed while we started turning our attention back to the couple about to step into our food.

"So, will you go to the bonfire with me?" He asked, hair messed up and covered in red confetti from the elaborate performance. Most people at our table gasped at hearing him ask her that. She smiled in response.

"Yes, of course!" She threw her arms around his neck and gave him the biggest teen rom-com kiss I'd ever seen. After the cheering stopped, he led her back down and kissed her hand before leaving. Somehow, she had ended up with the rose in her hand and set it next to her plate. I finished up my lunch while trying to ignore everyone clamoring for her attention. This was honestly a totally cheesy move and not even in a good way. Peer pressuring someone into accepting a date with you was not my idea of good communication.

It was very embarrassing to just watch them from the ground level, I thought. At least with this, everyone will have something other than me to talk about for a while.

I started going to class early, just to make sure I got there on time and to have some quiet. A headache was starting to pulse in my forehead and temples and the noise was making it worse. I was acutely aware that someone was behind me and glanced back to see that it was a guy. I moved to the side to let him by and he stopped.

"Oh, hey, you're Cora, aren't you?" He asked and my hackles went up. Something was very wrong with this situation.

"Yeah. What's your name?" I asked, turning to see he was standing very close to me.

"I'm Jay. Nice to meet you. Let's go to class together." He said and I did not like how he phrased it like an order.

"No, thanks. I'd rather walk alone." I said as I tried to walk away and he cornered me on the wall.

"I wasn't asking." He grinned and smelled like Axe. I gagged and reached for my pocket knife when he pinned my hand to the wall. This was not good. He had me cornered and no one was around.

"Let me go." I ordered and he laughed, bringing his face closer and smelling my hair.

"No. I don't think I will. "

He had done this whole romantic charade in front of everyone at Camp and still felt empty. He had taken an idea from one of his mother's favorite American films and it had been a huge hit. He watched Danny the whole time and saw her start to smile, fully under his spell.

Oh, well, he had got a date out of that deal.

One thing had bothered him, though, and it was that new girl again. She hadn't reacted at all to his elaborate serenade and everyone else had. She had, honestly, looked quite bored the whole time. He shook his head as he proceeded to finish his lunch. Maybe something was wrong with her, he thought. Everyone else always loved it when he performed.

As he watched everyone start getting up, he noticed that she started walking off by herself. He started checking to see if he was ready for their next music class when he realized that he had left his guitar and sheet music in the Big House that morning.

"Hey, I'll be back. I have to go get something." He announced as he got to his feet. He jogged back to find it and was on his way back to the amphitheater for class when he heard a male voice nearby.

"-Oh, come on. It'll be fun."

"I said 'no.' Now, excuse me." A girl's voice. That did not sound good and Rio slowed to a stop, leaning around the wall to see what was happening. It was Goldilocks again, but she was being blocked by Jay from Cabin 6. Rio already knew that this was a bad situation and decided to stay to see if she needed help. He saw that Jay had one of his arms pinning her hand to the wall and the other blocking her escape. Rio felt his fists clench and quietly set his guitar against the wall, ready to run in.

"Now, I never said you could go." The boy smiled and leaned his head down toward her face.

He never even got there. Rio saw her jaw clench and she used her good sense to kick him in the groin before running. He dropped quickly and yelled "You damn prude!"

"I said no!" She ran and Rio caught her by the arms. She looked up at him, completely terrified. Her hands shook under his and he realized that she was probably scared out of her mind. She snatched her arms away and dropped into a fighting stance.

"Whoa, what happened?" He asked, letting her know that she was safe.

"He- he tried to touch me. I didn't want him to." She responded, straightening back up. Rio nodded.

"Go get Chiron. I'll handle this strisciamento." She nodded and ran off while Rio turned to the boy starting to get up. Rio cracked his knuckles and walked over to the boy moaning in pain. Jay looked at him and his brown eyes widened with realization.

"You've gotta help me, man. She just attacked me outta nowhere." He tried to step toward Rio and Rio had him pinned to the wall in three seconds.

"Really? From what I saw, it was the other way around." Jay was about his height and built like an ox, which worried Rio a little bit. But, the fight was balanced because Rio was righteously angry and had surprise on his side. He had also been wanting to do this to Jay for a while, which is why he was being more aggressive than usual.

"So, you like to corner ladies, Jay? Let's see how you like it." When Jay's eyes narrowed, Rio cocked his hand back for a hit.

"No, you don't get it. She's the daughter of Eros. She came onto me and-" That was all he had time to say before Rio punched him straight in the nose with an open fist.

"Now, that is the biggest load of skata I've ever heard." Rio felt his nose crack and kept Jay pinned. "If you ever try to touch anyone without their consent again, I will personally break more than your nose. Capisci?" Rio asked him in a deep growl as the blood flowed freely from his nose and he dug his wrist harder into his throat. Jay yelled in pain and nodded.

"Ok, ok, I get it!" He struggled against Rio's hands. There was a small hand that grabbed at Rio's shoulder and he looked down.

"Rio, back off. He's had enough." He saw that it was Cora, out of breath and trying to pull him back. He released Jay, who fell to the ground. Chiron galloped in and took a quick survey of the situation.

"Rio, thank you for holding him still. Is everyone ok?" He asked, coming closer.

"I'm not." Jay raised his hand, to which both Rio and Cora unanimously responded with "We didn't ask you!"

Chiron nodded and hauled Jay up to his feet.

"Do you have anything to say, Jay?" He glared at him, obviously disapproving.

"I'm sorry." Jay muttered, staring at his blood-stained shoes.

Chiron took him out and Rio hung back with Cora, keeping his throbbing hand out of her view.

"Are you okay?" He asked, lowering his voice to a gentle tone. She looked up and nodded.

"Thanks. I guess I owe you one for that." She looked like she was still shaking and he walked over to get his guitar from the ground.

"You don't owe me a thing. It was worth it to see you kick him like that. Did you use my name just now?" He said, strapping it back on. She smiled a little and started walking back out.

"Still. I feel bad that I trashed you in class and you just came swooping in to help. And, so what if I did, Abercrombie?" She shoved her shaking hands into her pockets as she spoke.

"You did not 'trash' me at anything. I was having an off day." He snorted indignantly at the nickname.

"Right. I think the better term is 'royally kicked your ass.' You should put ice on that hand if you want to play this week,

Romeo." She grinned, jogging off to find her class before he had a chance to respond.

9 798330 590117